ON
A SLIDE
OF
LIGHT

ON A SLIDE OF LIGHT

✻

Greta Woodrew

MACMILLAN PUBLISHING CO., INC.

New York

COLLIER MACMILLAN PUBLISHERS

London

Macmillan Publishing Co., Inc.
866 Third Avenue, New York, N.Y. 10022
Collier Macmillan Canada, Ltd.

Library of Congress Cataloging in Publication Data
Woodrew, Greta.
   On a slide of light.
   1. Psychical research.   2. Occult sciences.
I. Title.
BF1999.W696   133.8   80-24577
ISBN 0-02-631390-1

10 9 8 7 6 5 4 3 2 1
Designed by Jack Meserole
Printed in the United States of America

To all perceptive interpreters of
the world of human, planetary, galactic, and
intergalactic observable experiences, my book
is dedicated.

To my patient, gentle, protective, and
ever-supportive husband, Dick—"Dear Ezra"—
for his steadfast work in
the realms of interaction in countless fields
of newly acquired knowledge, my heart
is dedicated.

To those who will be present,
aware, and unafraid at the coming
of the gattae, my work
is dedicated.

CONTENTS

ACKNOWLEDGMENTS

Particular thanks and overwhelming gratitude go first and fore-most to my husband, Dick, without whose constant understanding and persistent research, *On a Slide of Light* might well have remained a mission incomplete instead of a fait accompli.

I am ever indebted to each and every one of my four children for their support, concern, encouragement, and unflagging interest and participation.

A special acknowledgment to special friends, Jill and Marilynn, for their respective free-lance editing and proofreading of many, many hours.

To my staff at Woodrew Services, and to Dick's partner, Mike— for "keeping the home fires burning"—my gratefulness is enormous.

To the researchers and scientists in the Frontiers of Physics who extended a vote of confidence and enthusiasm, my sincere appre-ciation.

And finally . . . to my fine feathered friends in the Ogatta group . . . I say bless them all. I hope this small effort of a very *human* being is satisfactory to them.

AUTHOR'S NOTE

There are many sound waves around us we do not normally hear and of which we are totally unaware. When we turn on a radio, we are able to tune into these waves, and the finer the radio receiver, the greater the number of waves we are able to monitor.

In the same way, many of the ideas discussed in this book deal with waves that our normal receivers—our five senses—do not ordinarily pick up. Extending the analogy one step further, all of us actually are the "radio." Some of us have broader bands than others. After two decades of research and involvement in parapsychological work, my "radio" is perhaps more finely tuned than most. For this reason, I want to share with you some of the waves my antennae have picked up and which yours possibly missed.

It is common practice in a book of this kind to set forth the thesis at the outset. I therefore boldly claim that my radio receives waves whose existence is not even suspected by the average person. I have the rest of the book in which to explain *how* and *why* my radio works.

If the story I am about to reveal were just my own, it would not be necessary for me to try to "bend" your minds as I have frequently bent stainless steel spoons with my mind. But I have been advised that even at the risk of disrupting my private life, my experiences should become a matter of public record, because certain vital changes are starting to occur that will escalate and affect every living creature on the planet. Therefore this story is every bit as much yours as it is mine.

On a Slide of Light presents material that may seem as hard to perceive as those elusive sound waves. It is my hope that you will be open to new concepts and not reject the "radio" summarily. In this spirit I invite you to explore some bold new hypotheses and to ride on a slide of light with me into the mind, the heart, the consciousness—the Cosmos.

G.W.

ON
A SLIDE
OF
LIGHT

1

Stepping Forward

MOST PEOPLE find real only those things they can perceive and project through their five senses. The story you are about to read deals with realities that extend far beyond these limited wavelengths. It is a tale that must be told because it involves certain imminent changes that will affect every human being on this globe.

The story may strike you as alien—bizarre. Frankly, it strikes me that way too. I lead a very active, fairly conventional, and utterly credible life in the Connecticut suburbs, a life that is shared with a wonderful husband and four grown children. As president of an executive search firm, I fill middle- and upper-management positions in major corporations around the country.

Surely anyone who runs a home, raises a family, supervises a business has to be very much in touch with everyday reality. But my experience has taught me that there are realities awesomely beyond our daily sense-bound lives. Because of this experience, I am prepared to risk the precious privacy of my personal life and to jeopardize my position in the mainstream of our society.

As I approach fifty, I look with some pride on my accomplishments as a researcher, business person, teacher, wife and mother. A Phi Beta Kappa Achievement Award and an honorary LL.D. substantiate this pride, as do the attainments of the other members of my family. My husband Dick has been president of his own company for many years. As for our four children, Alan has his M.B.A. from Lehigh, Jonathan and Jill are Princeton graduates, and our youngest, Ann, will graduate shortly from Dartmouth.

Those are the dimensions of my life that need no explanation.

But the *other* dimension—this story—concerns my contact with ETI: Extra Terrestrial Intelligence. It is the dimension I have come to refer to as "out there."

My adventures with ETI began four years ago. The initial contacts took place under laboratory conditions with the guidance of a leading medical doctor and scientist. It was my impression that once I left his lab, I would also leave ETI behind. But this was not to be the case. Once I exercised my free will in allowing extraterrestrials into my life, they quickly became a regular part of my experienced reality.

I could be sitting at my desk at—let us say—10 A.M., getting ready to phone a client about a prospect. As I dialed the number I would again glance at the clock and to my confusion it would read 10:45. Somewhere between the time I reached for the phone and the time I started to dial, an interval that should have been less than a second, a full forty-five minutes had elapsed.

What was happening? What did these peculiar lapses of time and attention mean? They were the beginning of what was to be a continuing dialogue with ETI, transcending time and space and the third dimension.

In the days that followed my laboratory introduction to the Cosmos, the other members of my family were included in conversations with the ETI. Our visitors informed us that they came from another civilization in another solar system located astronomically on the Messier List at M-92, with a further identification clue of 0-47. Its name is Ogatta and it is part of a binary or twin-star system which comprises what they call a "jorpah" (and we call a solar system) of five planets in another galaxy:

Ogatta, Oshan, Archa, Mennon, and Tchauvi.

The gentle, often whimsical, but always enlightening inhabitants of Ogatta have become honored guests and welcome callers in our home. From their first contact in 1976 to their most recent one, their visits never fail to boggle our minds. They provide a constant stream of cosmic serendipity.

What is the purpose of these visits? It seems that they have chosen me to be one of their channels or conduits through whom they impart their messages to those who choose to listen. Why me? I do not know. I feel that I am a highly unlikely choice to relay these vital messages. But they obviously do not agree.

My experiences with the Ogatta group have been stimulating, educational, and alternately frustrating, exhilarating, mystifying, bewildering, and gratifying. For my husband and my four adult children, who have been scribes, witnesses, protectors, and students, the seeing was much of the believing. But for you, who may not have had such experiences, I have only words to open your minds— and a vocabulary which is often inadequate to describe things and events for which we as yet have no words.

I shall never forget my first encounter with an extraterrestrial. I was standing in a long shadowy tunnel with a manlike being who had the most marvelous eyes I have ever seen—golden, human, deeply compassionate. There were two entities with him, both with those same wonderful eyes. They all shared a rather birdlike quality, due in part to the shape of the upper lip. They seemed to be guarding the tunnel.

When I tried to speak to them, to ask who they were and where they came from, the first one stepped forward. He was answering me but his lips never moved. He was communicating telepathically and—amazingly—I could understand every word!

The being's name was Shames, he told me, and he and his companions had been sent from Ogatta, many light-ages away. As he gave me this message, he held me with his eyes. Again I was struck by how unbelievably beautiful they were. Beautiful . . . beautiful . . . beautiful . . .

A second later, I was back in a more familiar world with a more familiar face—my husband's—at my side. We had been visiting the renowned physician and psi researcher, Dr. Andrija Puharich, and it was he who had guided me into that tunnel where I met my first visitor from the Ogatta group. We were later to learn that Shames had been sent from Ogatta, but actually came from Mennon.

On the way home from that never to be forgotten session, Dick and I talked about my unlikely encounter. How could we explain to our family, or to anyone else, the existence of this entity whom I had seen face to face, so vividly and in such minute detail? In actuality a new world was opening up to us. I sensed, too, that I would be expected to communicate things I had seen, to share the information that I knew would be forthcoming. I wondered how well I could live a "normal" life with such manifestations surrounding me.

Four years have gone by since I met Shames in that tunnel. Since then, I have had to continue being a pragmatic businesswoman, to learn to walk a fine line to maintain my balance and credibility with friends, clients, and professional associates. They, like you, would probably say "*NO!*" to the possibility of communications with extraterrestrials. But if that is what you are tempted to say, let me remind you of how many things in our twentieth-century world were once thought impossible but have come into being.

When I was a child, my grandmother used to read stories to me. Among my favorites were Jules Verne's marvelous fantasies, the forerunners of today's science fiction. Could Verne have foreseen when he wrote *20,000 Leagues under the Sea* in 1873 that modern scientists and technologists would develop what he called diving bells, aqualungs, submarines, television? Did he know when he wrote *From the Earth to the Moon* in 1865 that men would actually make that journey in the very next century?

Verne himself would probably be astounded to find that so many of his imaginative tales and terms have come true. And what would he—who sent Phileas Fogg around the world in an unbelievable eighty days to win a bet—think of astronaut John Glenn who orbited the same planet less than a hundred years later in a mere four hours and fifty-six minutes? Verne's science fiction has become our present-day reality.

Today's young people, who have grown up with space flights and lunar landings and communications satellites, do not find it strange to think of life on other planets or in other galaxies. I hope that you will be able to put aside your own doubts and become open to the possibility that the experiences I am about to relate are not only real but have a significant, even a crucial bearing on your life.

But how can I—or anyone else—share an experience with someone who lacks the framework to understand and cope with it? People know only what they can visualize, imagine, or sense. Yet I had encountered an entity who claimed to be from another civilization in another dimension and solar system. Had anyone else ever been presented with a dilemma like this? Of course. Many famous names in history have faced credibility problems.

When Columbus proved that the world was round, he too created a dilemma. The people to whom he brought this information had no frame of reference in which to place it, so they did the logical thing—they discarded it. And Galileo was placed under house arrest for three years because he proposed that the Earth was not the center of the universe, but rather a part of a system that revolved around the Sun. Was this the sort of resistance I would meet? Or, worse than resistance, would I face hostility and ridicule?

Perhaps not, Dick reassured me. People have been facing this sort of problem from the time men first ventured from their homes to discover new places and people. Can you imagine the first encounter between peoples of different races? The shock must have been as great as it would be today, if someone from a small tribal village in Africa were to be plunged suddenly in the center of New York City and then went home and tried to describe it to his friends. Man has constantly been jolted out of his provincial niches by new technologies as he has traveled from his early beginnings to the twentieth century.

I feel that my interaction with beings from another dimension has been no different. These experiences have jolted my family and me out of our comfortable niches and given us information of such a nature that I am compelled to pass it along.

My friends from the Ogatta group are concerned about the future. They tell of changes that will alter our planet and our lives. Many of the changes they speak of are already being reported in our newspapers; some are happening in the vicinity of your own homes. The transitions are all there if we would but see and make the connections. The short-range projections that the ETI have divulged so far have all been right on target. I have no doubt they will be equally accurate in their long-range forecasts. When I first suggested in public appearances a few years ago that climatic changes and quaking and shaking were imminent, people called me a "doom-and-gloomer." Today, they merely nod their heads in understanding of what ETI had originally foretold to me.

Let me tell you about something one of my extraterrestrial friends, Tauri, revealed to me in June of 1978. Andrija Puharich, who has also seen and talked with members of the Ogatta group, had mentioned something about the Middle East, which brought up the subject of Israel. Listen to what Tauri said to us:

Israel has been used as a football before. There is *more* trouble in a place you do not consider . . . a trouble spot where Israel is concerned. *It* is more of a trouble spot than any other. That is Iran! There is one man who is—as they say in your language—a megalomaniac.

I want to tell you—keep your eye on him.

It was another fifteen months before we realized how right Tauri was. I doubt anyone could have foreseen at that time that the government of Iran would undergo so many upheavals.

Historian William Irwin Thompson once said: "Experts are right only about what has been and not what can be." The ETI point the way to what *will* be. They have nudged us into discovering "Universes beyond matter in the cosmic reaches of the spirit." It is not enough merely to listen to the prelude to the symphony that is playing. The Ogatta group are inviting—no, urging—us to be part of the orchestra. In fact, the overture has already begun.

The music it is playing will not always be joyful. Some of the melodies will break our hearts. In an altered state of consciousness, I have witnessed a devastation to our planet which is coming in my own lifetime—in the next several decades. It has started already. The saga of Mount St. Helens is only a harbinger of things to come. Subjected to those unforgettable prophetic glimpses of the future, I wept for humanity as I viewed the Scenario in its entirety:

Hurricanes. Floods. Super magnetic storms. Droughts. Earthquakes. Volcanoes. Tidal waves that buried whole cities and their populations beneath walls of water. People dying of thirst and hunger. Children with burns on their bodies. Animals with their hair scorched and their eyes glazed. Fish with gills slit and clogged. Birds with wings that cannot carry them into flight. I witnessed with horror what appeared to be the devastation of our beautiful planet.

My extradimensional view of these terrifying events began during the first meeting with Shames, that marvelous creature with the golden eyes who entered my consciousness on a December day in 1976. Since then I have met fourteen of the Ogatta group—from

wise, wonderful Shames to the impish, kindhearted, incredibly en-
lightened Tauri who prefers to manifest as a child.

This is a very personal story. I think of it as an "Ah! book"—
a rather special category that the British writer, Vernon Sproxton,
described as one that induces fundamental change in the reader's
consciousness. As Sproxton puts it, " 'Ah! books' touch upon the
nerve center of the whole being so that the reader receives an almost
palpable physical shock. They widen his sensibilities in such a way
that he is able to look upon familiar things as though he is seeing
them for the first time."

I can't guarantee that this book will live up to that definition,
but I am fairly certain that it will provide some "Ah! moments, Ah!
thoughts, Ah! concepts," and most of all, "Ah! explanations."

Although I often have had doubts about telling this story, I
have been reassured by the studies of others who have cause to believe in life beyond this limited planet of ours. Are you aware, for
example, that the United States has established a program to Search
for Extraterrestrial Intelligence, SETI? The Soviet Union has set up
a similar program to Communicate with Extraterrestrial Intelligence, CETI. A report prepared for the Committee on Science and
Technology of the U.S. House of Representatives, Ninety-fifth Congress, in October 1977, revealed that no less than nine searches for
ETI had already been undertaken by both countries, five by the
United States and four by the U.S.S.R. In that same year, the Japanese announced their intent to become active in the SETI. The
formation of a committee to study the matter has also been a subject
of some high-level deliberations at the United Nations.

A quote from Tauri on the subject in August 1978:

Let's put it this way; there are those who search for extraterrestrials.
There are those who talk to extraterrestrials. Isn't it marvelous that your
United Nations is now discussing how much to allocate for something that
they did not believe *existed* not that long ago! I think that's wondrous—
I think that's progress—I think that's very human.

Because of my involvement with the more highly evolved and
benevolent entities from Ogatta, I have agreed to assist them in a
very human way in bringing their message into public view. My

visitors want all of us to be aware of the changes to come, changes that for the most part are already in motion. They ask me to urge as many as possible to examine the effects of mind over matter. They caution all of us to understand the principles that influence our universe.

For the present, those of the Ogatta group deal only with a selected handful of human beings—like myself. They have trained us as channels to handle their communications and pass their directions along. (*"Directions,* not *directives,"* they emphasize.) While they have the ability to manifest themselves on the Earth in their natural forms and shapes, their higher vibrations would damage our frailer bodies. Goblets shatter when sopranos energize and amplify their notes. Genetic damage occurs when radiations bombard the body beyond one's ability to handle them (as occurred at the Love Canal). Similarly, our nervous systems would suffer irreparable damage if we currently tried to handle Ogatta-level energies.

We must be properly prepared. Those within the Ogatta jorpah have no wish to destroy things as they are, but rather to create new structures with which we will cope successfully in our threatened world.

In the not too distant future we will share the Ogatta technology, but we must first become capable of tuning into the bands on which the information is stored. We will glean much new data as we move into new patterns of existence in what may best be described as a fifth-dimensional world.

I am telling all this at the urging of the Ogatta group because these are the first rungs on the ladder to the Cosmos and back again. Those who wish to join in the climb will adjust and heighten their awareness day by day. ETI tells us that we are destined to inhabit a different world. Before the turn of this century ". . . what was, will no longer be."

The transition has already begun.

2

Fate and Fatality

H O W M A N Y T I M E S do we hear ourselves say, "What a coincidence?" It was certainly a recurrent phrase in my vocabulary during my younger years. But at what point do we stop and say, "This *has* to be more than a coincidence!" At what point do we begin to entertain other possibilities, to think that there may be more to life than what we perceive with our limited five senses, to wonder if the Nobel Prize physicist Wolfgang Pauli was not right when he called coincidences "the visible traces of untraceable principles"?

That moment came for me in 1961. The month was August. Some friends of ours had asked us to join them in celebrating their wedding anniversary with a night on the town in New York. The husband's parents, who lived in Florida, had just flown up north and were staying at the Delmonico Hotel. We agreed to stop by for a visit before going out to dinner.

When we arrived at their suite, we found another guest already there—a woman named Mary, a friend of a friend, whom they had been anxious to meet. We chatted pleasantly about a number of things, I've long since forgotten what. I do recall, however, that in the course of our conversation, Mary, who worked as a secretary for a major corporation in New York, mentioned that she was a psychic.

I was skeptical and I'm sure my skepticism showed, but Mary, far from being troubled by my reaction, asked me if I had ever had a "reading."

"No," I said, trying not to be rude. "I don't believe in that sort of thing."

Mary smiled and said, "Give me your wedding band."

I refused, explaining that I never took it off my finger. But I was

9

curious about Mary's claim that by simply holding an object that belonged to me, she would be able to see into my life. I had heard of this ability, which is called psychometry, but I did not believe anyone really possessed it. Nevertheless, I gave Mary my watch and listened in awe as she began to recite all sorts of details about my past and present life.

At first I thought a joke was being played on me—that Mary had been clued in by our host and hostess and knew in advance what to say. But I quickly abandoned that theory. Mary was bringing up matters known only to me. Not even my husband was aware of some of the information she rattled off so knowingly. And our friends and their relatives were completely in the dark.

It would have taken expert research to dig out the incidents that Mary described from my past. And I doubt if any researcher could have unearthed so many details about my mother, father, brothers, and grandmother. I was absolutely speechless.

Mary then went on to do the same thing with each of the other people in the room, her revelations about past and present episodes all right on target. It seemed as if she had thoroughly researched every one of us gathered there that evening.

Just before we left, I went into the bedroom to comb my hair. Mary followed me. When I looked at her quizzically, she said, "Your life will change very, very drastically in eight months. There will be a death. In the long run, *your* life will be the most deeply affected."

My heart started to pound. This woman whom I had only just met had been so remarkably accurate about everything else she told me that I had no choice but to believe her.

"What do you see?" I demanded. "My husband? One of my children?"

"No, no. Not your husband or any of your children," she replied.

"Who then? And why will I be more affected than anyone else? Will it be one of my parents? Or brothers? Who?"

Mary looked at me intently and said in a very positive tone, "Your father-in-law will meet an untimely death and *your* life-style will undergo the greatest change of all."

I will never forget that sentence as long as I live. I adored my father-in-law. In fact, Dick and I had built our home right next to his parents. I knew I would be deeply grieved if anything happened to either of my in-laws. But Dick was his father's business partner, best friend, fellow sports fan, only son. How could *I* be "more affected" than he—or, for that matter, his mother, married for thirty-four years? I fled the room in tears, murmuring a hasty goodbye to our friend's mother and father. They seemed bewildered by my anxiety but tactfully refrained from asking its cause.

I recovered sufficiently to enjoy our evening out, but my conversation with Mary was still very much alive in my mind. On the way home in the car, I couldn't resist blurting out Mary's prediction to my friend as we sat together in the back seat. I begged her never to repeat it. I was determined not to let my husband, or anyone else, know what I had been told.

Mary, however, had told our friend's parents about our exchange. They called me the very next morning, not only to thank us for dropping by to see them, but to apologize for "that ridiculous prediction Mary told us she gave you." They were obviously embarrassed by the episode. To ease their discomfort, I made light of the whole affair.

In reality, Mary's prediction had left me with mixed feelings of indignation and apprehension. What rubbish! How dare she say such things? Who but a lunatic would believe them? I knew I was crazy to think about it, much less dwell upon it. Untimely death for a man who had never known a sick day in his life? It was absurd, and I was determined to put it out of my mind. But I never could; it simply refused to go away.

In the weeks and months that followed our meeting with Mary, I painstakingly relived that evening's events. I came to the conclusion that she had definitely not had any previous knowledge of my existence. Our friend's parents had not even known we were going to stop by on our way to dinner.

I had to admit that Mary's facts and figures, names, dates, and places were all correct. I had no idea how she knew so much, but I had to concede that she did know an incredible amount about me. This made it all the more possible that she might be correct in her prediction. It was a frightening thought and I couldn't help being haunted by it.

I started to study my father-in-law's every move. If he so much as sneezed or coughed, I was panic-stricken. I became extremely nervous but steadfastly refused to tell my ever patient husband why. Two months, four months, six months passed, and there was never a day that I didn't think of that dreadful prediction of Dad's "untimely death."

One day an artist friend of mine, Irma, stopped in for a visit and found me lying on the couch, sobbing. I am not a crier by nature and Irma, who had never seen me in tears, put her arms around me and asked what was wrong. Despite all the promises I had made to myself to keep quiet, I told her the whole story.

Irma's eyes flashed angrily. "That's sheer rubbish!" she exclaimed. "Pay no attention to that woman! Forget everything she said!"

I wiped my eyes, grinned sheepishly, and agreed that it *did* sound rather farfetched. I assured Irma that I would put Mary and her psychic statements out of my mind once and for all.

Eight months passed and despite my promise to Irma and to myself, I still couldn't shake off the memory of that monstrous prediction. April arrived and my father-in-law's fifty-seventh birthday was only a few days away. Dad never worked on Fridays during the spring and summer months. He preferred to take his vacation by stretching his weekends with an extra day, which he spent playing golf, puttering in his garden, and being with his family. Another Friday pastime was a special late-afternoon walk with me.

That particular Friday was no different from the others. Dad set out for the golf course as usual, first thing in the morning. I knew he would be striding briskly along the fairways by the time I ran down the hill to bring my mother-in-law a book she had wanted to borrow. To my surprise, however, my father-in-law was not at the golf club. He was sitting in his bedroom looking alarmingly pale. He had gone off for his usual game, he explained, but had felt so rotten after nine holes that he decided to come home and relax instead of playing a second nine. Dad looked terrible. He said nothing about being in pain, but it was obvious that he was not his usual self.

My mother-in-law was clearly upset by his condition, and the two of us instantly agreed that we should call a doctor, much to my father-in-law's disgust. The doctor wasn't in the house two minutes when he called for an ambulance to take Dad to the hospital. He did not know precisely what was wrong, he told us, but there was no question in his mind that this man was terribly ill.

I suppose none of us should have been surprised that Dad had never complained of any pain. He was a true Taurus—a bull of a man. Big voice, big frame, big heart. His threshold of pain was so high that once, when he was using a buzz saw to cut some logs, he gave himself a severe gash on the leg and barely noticed it. Anyone else would have felt weak and sick for days after an accident like that, but he was impervious to such things.

But now his wife and son, the rest of the family, even the doctor seemed to feel that this strong patriarch would not pull through. I, on the other hand, was convinced that Dad would make it. Although he slipped into a coma and was put onto an ice-sheet, every time I walked into his room he would open his eyes and say a few brief, but extremely lucid, words to me. No one could account for these miraculous returns to consciousness but those who witnessed them wept in disbelief.

Three days after Dad was stricken, the doctor solemnly informed us that he would not live through the night. When I heard the news, I raced down the hospital corridor to his room, where he lay in a comatose state. Standing by his bedside, I looked down at the wonderful human being who was my father-in-law, screaming mentally: *"Live!"*

With that, Dad opened his large blue eyes; I couldn't help noticing how clear they were. Bolting upright despite all the tubes connected to him, he grabbed me and pulled me down over his chest in a ferocious bear hug. He said only one sentence—a private message that had deep meaning for both of us—then collapsed back onto the ice-sheet in a coma. Four hours later, he was gone. I was still the only one totally unprepared for the news. I was shocked and devastated by his death.

I look back now with genuine amazement that neither then, nor at any time during Dad's illness, did I recall the prediction that had been given to me the previous August. Although I had brooded incessantly on the prospect of his death for eight long months, when he was finally stricken, my conscious memory of the prediction mysteriously vanished. It did not return until ten days after Dad's funeral.

My husband had been forced to throw himself into the task of reorganizing his sizable business so it could continue to function without the leadership of his partner and best friend. Dick literally had no time to mourn his father's passing. It was more than a week after the funeral before he finally faced up to the loss we had all suffered. The release came in a flood, and as I took him in my arms, I found a release of sorts. In that instant I remembered Mary's eight-month-old prediction, and a feeling of peace came over me. "It was meant to be," I told Dick softly. "It couldn't have happened any other way."

When I explained why I believed this, Dick was dubious. "I love you for trying to ease the pain," he said, "but I simply cannot accept what you are saying."

"There are others who know," I said quietly. "Four people know the prediction."

He stared skeptically at me and demanded to know who the four people were.

"My friend, her parents-in-law, and Irma," I told him.

It was a little after midnight but Dick insisted that I call one of them.

"Now?"

"Yes, now."

I dialed my friend who spoke to Dick and confirmed the story. Still not completely convinced, he asked for her in-laws' phone number and called them in Florida.

At the other end of the wire, the gentle, sleepy voice of my friend's mother-in-law said, "Oh, Dick, when I heard about your father's death, all I could think of was that horrible prediction that Mary made to Greta last August."

Dick sat transfixed. Then he collected himself and calmly asked for the name and telephone number of the mysterious psychic, Mary. We were given her office number, and the next day we called her and asked her to meet us during her lunch hour. I could already see that Dick's mourning was giving way to a new acceptance of his loss, a feeling that fate may have indeed played a hand in the events of the previous two weeks.

Although Mary remembered meeting us at the hotel suite, she confessed that she had no recollection of her prediction. Determined to refresh her memory, I repeated the story of that August encounter slowly and deliberately. As I did so, a conviction began to form in my heart that no *good* psychic would ever make such a prediction. I have never altered that conviction. It is cruel to burden anyone with the knowledge of an impending death.

As I finished recounting for Mary the events of our previous meeting at the Delmonico Hotel, I couldn't resist asking her the one question uppermost in my mind: "How in the world did you know?"

The next sixty seconds are etched in my very being. Mary stood up and walked slowly over to me. She looked deeply into my eyes for a long moment and smiled sadly. Putting her hand under my chin, she replied, "Why ask me? You are far more psychic than I."

With those words, the second half of Mary's prediction began to be fulfilled. Her statement prompted me to begin exploring my own psychic abilities and—as Mary had promised—my life has undergone some unexpected and highly dramatic changes.

3

Peering Inward

MARY'S WORDS, "You are far more psychic than I," rang a distinct bell.

As a child I had constantly heard the grownups around me say, "Greta has a vivid imagination." I grew tired of the refrain, so I learned to keep quiet about a lot of things that were very real to me but not to everyone around me.

At a very young age I realized that if you're living a conventional life but have experiences that are unconventional, you don't stand much chance of convincing your parents, friends, or teachers that the things you see and hear are real. When that happens, your options quickly become quite clear: you can either get into step with everyone else or march quietly to the sound of drums that beat only for you.

A dependent and docile child who is pushed to get into step invariably turns away from the world of the psyche and opts for becoming acceptable, thus joining the mainstream of humdrum existence. The child will live in the obvious physical universe so acceptable to the parent and will push away the reality of a psychic world to which the parent might not be privy. This is unfortunate because, in all too many instances, children with vivid imaginations possess a heightened sensitivity. Many of them have the ability to perceive the world around them through the sixth or intuitive sense that most adults don't exercise or have long since forgotten exists. Once children abandon that intuitive faculty they are seldom able to recreate, or even remember, it. A block of my psychic life was turned off for me when I was nine years old, and it was to be more than thirty years before the memory of the astral experiences of my childhood returned to me.

After my father-in-law's death, I was determined to find out more about the world of psi phenomena and to discover what—if any—role I was to play in it. But where was I to begin? I love to play games, particularly games of chance, so I started with a deck of cards. My aim was to try and separate the deck into blacks and reds without looking at the cards. The more I practiced, the better my percentages became. One day, twenty-six black cards and twenty-six red cards fell into place from a brand new deck shuffled by somebody else. The same division occurred repeatedly after that day. Once I tried the feat at the home of a highly skeptical IBM executive who promptly became one of my staunchest supporters.

Several of my friends urged me to visit the famous Parapsychological Laboratory that had been founded at Duke University by Dr. J. B. Rhine. There my abilities could be tested under scientifically controlled conditions. But I had no desire to be a laboratory guinea pig; nor did I want to be thrust into the public eye, so I always declined. Even when Dr. Rhine himself asked me to come to Duke, I refused.

Scientists claim that human beings use no more than 9 percent of their brains, but they have no doubt that the remaining 91 percent has a purpose. I agree with them. In ancient times, the unused portion of the brain was referred to as "the seat of intuition."

Now that I had decided to use it, my intutition seemed to be improving with practice. A case in point: when our friend Bishop James Pike was lost on an expedition in a remote part of the Israeli desert in 1969, I sent a telegram to his wife Diane to "look to a ledge." I sensed too that Jim would be found in a kneeling position. Many days later, a search party found Jim's body. He had died on his knees on a mountain ledge. Later, Diane Kennedy Pike wrote to tell me that several other psychics had picked up the same picture of her late husband.

My husband Dick was baffled by, but far from unappreciative of, my gifts. Ever the man of reason, he insisted that we be scientific in our game-playing. He suggested that we perform some telepathy experiments together and keep records of the results. I agreed, and thus began a series of games in which we tried to communicate mentally whenever we were separated by long distances. We kept our messages simple—a color, number, phrase, or brief thought.

Dick and I took turns acting as sender and receiver, and we were impressed at how often we succeeded in picking up each other's thoughts. We always sent our messages when we were either on land or water, but on one occasion, when Dick was planning a business trip to South Carolina, we decided to conduct our experiment while his plane was in the air. I was to be the receiver, and we set 9 P.M. as the precise time at which he would transmit a four-word message. The only restriction was that he had to send a thought totally divorced from anything connected with our home and children.

We had already worked out a foolproof system for our experiments. The sender would write down his message and hold it in his hand at the appointed time for a full five minutes. At the same time, the receiver would write down whatever message or impression he received. We would then slip our individual pieces of paper into envelopes, seal them, and open each other's envelopes simultaneously when we were together again.

When 9 P.M. rolled around on that particular evening, I was playing bridge with my mother-in-law. I was concentrating so hard on trying to make my Four-No-Trump bid that I totally forgot poor Dick sitting on the plane to South Carolina, concentrating for all he was worth. By the time I finished the hand and remembered him, it was 9:15. Our experiment period was officially over. I felt a little guilty, but it was too late to rectify the situation so I stopped worrying.

As I was getting ready for bed a few hours later, I began to think about something I had read regarding waves bouncing around in the air. A defunct television station's old programming, the article said, had suddenly appeared on people's screens long after the station had ceased its operations. Neither the station personnel nor any of the other experts the author had interviewed could explain why.

Perhaps Dick's message is still out there somewhere, I thought as I undressed. Why not try to catch it? I glanced at my clock and saw that it was exactly 12:05. I "blanked my mind," as one must do in order to pick up an impression, and a message appeared in my consciousness: talents are many for you. It was five words, rather than the agreed-upon four, and it sounded a bit silly, but I wrote it down anyway, sealed it in an envelope, and went to bed.

Three days later Dick arrived home from South Carolina and handed me his envelope. The message inside read: Use your many talents.

Off the record, parapsychologists at the American Society for Psychic Research labeled our experiment a "near miss," but considering the circumstances under which the message was transmitted, I think it was amazingly accurate!

Over the next two or three years, Dick and I embarked on a self-imposed program of study. We tackled everything we thought might be helpful to our understanding of psi. We read about, and I learned to see, auras—the emanations from people's bodies that reveal their physical and emotional states. The aura is really the weathervane of the soul and of the body. Pythagoras (580–500 B.C.) referred to auras as "luminous bodies." We also delved further into psychometry, which we had first witnessed when Mary took my watch in her hand and told me all about myself. I had not understood it at the time, but I eventually discovered that I too could do it.

Much later, I read of the work of two acclaimed Russian scientists, Dr. Genady Sergeyev and Dr. Viktor Adamenko, who have unlocked the mystery of psychometry. As the scientists were able to demonstrate, human beings radiate energy which is soaked up and stored by the objects around us. Since energy can never be destroyed, our energy imprints are preserved for all eternity. In addition, when an object absorbs energy, the magnetic characteristics of its molecules change and the object becomes a natural magnetic recorder. This is the same principle of magnetic induction used in the disc storage of data in the computer industry. Magnetic induction changes the medium on which the data is stored.

The Russian scientists are currently at a stage where they can recover electrical information from objects and get a computer printout, but they are still unable to interpret the printout. However, there are certain individuals whose extrasensory awareness allows them both to receive and understand such information.

The knowledge I acquired through our program of study helped me to recognize—and expose—a number of psychic charlatans. To me this brand of dishonesty is particularly reprehensible, not only because it dupes innocent people, but because it stops reasonable adults—including, for a long while, me—from understanding what good sensitives are capable of doing.

In the course of our explorations into psi, I met one woman who was to have a most profound influence on my learning—Caroline Chapman. "The dean of mediums," as she is called in psychic circles, was already quite old and her eyesight was failing when we met. No one had ever "read" for her successfully, but she had given her own amazing readings to famous people the world over. Lester Pearson, then prime minister of Canada, consulted her frequently, and the day I met her she had just given a private reading to Charles de Gaulle.

Chappy was a tiny, dynamic woman with a sparkling wit. I came to adore her. I also came to "read" successfully for her to her never-ending delight. Once when Chappy was spending the weekend at our home along with poet Jean Wallace, she asked me if I had ever attempted table-tilting. I hadn't, and with the enthusiasm of a teenager, she exclaimed, "Well, let's give it a try!"

We all sat down, put our fingertips on a heavy, glass-topped, free-form table, and waited. The room was dimly lit. I cannot claim that I saw or felt the table move, but I do know that it was the night of my first experience with automatic writing. All of a sudden my hand started to move, with no effort on my part, in a writing motion. Chappy quickly placed a pen in my fingers and put a piece of paper in front of me. I wrote rapidly for a second and then flung what I had written away from me onto the floor.

We retrieved the paper after the session and found that it contained what appeared to be the signature of my father-in-law, who by then had been dead for almost two years. The following Monday morning we took the slip of paper to the bank and compared it with the signature that had been on Dad's old vault card. They were identical. I found the whole experience so unsettling that I determined never to attempt table-tilting again. The paraphernalia of the "spiritual community" is really not for me.

As Chappy's health and eyesight waned, she beseeched me to see some of her clients and relieve her of at least part of her workload. At that stage of her life, she was forced to do readings to support herself. I had vowed, however, never to take money for any psychic work. Since I know that people tend to minimize anything they get for nothing, I decided instead to ask them to make a donation to their favorite charity or, if they didn't have one, to mine—by way of payment.

I used that system until Chappy died and I then stopped giving readings to anyone at all. During that time I raised thousands of dollars for all sorts of charitable institutions and provided all clients with tax deductions in the bargain.

The hardest thing I had to learn as a "reader" was to say, "I'm sorry, I just do not get anything today," to someone who might have traveled hundreds of miles to see me. During this period I visited a great many self-described mediums myself and found too many of them to be frauds. I had long ago sworn that I would never fool either myself or the people who sought my help.

It really isn't too hard to "fake it"—to look for a clue in the eyes of the person sitting opposite you and to go forward on a theme when the eyes confirm a "hit." But as I found to my dismay, human beings are peculiar. They would rather be deceived—if the deception contains the information they are looking for—than be told the truth.

When I was honest enough to admit that I couldn't get anything, the people who came to me were apt to become demanding and abusive. "What do you mean you can't get anything?" they'd snap. "Why, I've traveled a long distance to see you, young lady!"

Sometimes I wished I was as sure about even a few things as so many of these people seemed to be about everything.

The last straw came with a telephone call. At the time it made me angry, but in retrospect it strikes me funny. The phone rang and a long-distance operator asked for me. In another moment a male voice came on the line and announced, "This is a senator in Washington. Can you help me?"

"*A* senator?" I said, "Do you have a name? And how did you get to me?"

"Never mind all that," was the abrupt reply. "My wife inherited a very unusual pin from my great-grandmother, an heirloom with great sentimental value. She lost it, and I am hoping you can find it. Can you?"

I told the senator that I had never tried to locate a missing object over the phone before, but I also felt compelled to ask him if his wife did any gardening.

"Yes," he said.

"Has she planted any pansies recently?"

"She has a gorgeous pansy garden," was the excited reply.

"Tell her to go look near the little pansy-faces," I said, "and I do believe she will find her pin lying there."

The senator's excitement mounted.

"I can see the garden from my window," he told me. "I'll go look myself. Hold on!"

He put down the phone with an abrupt clatter.

A few expensive moments later, the senator was back on the line. By now he was so excited that he was barely coherent. "It's here in my hand! It was there where you said! This is amazing! Amazing!"

I was delighted that I had been able to "see" the precious heirloom and thrilled to have brought so much pleasure to this nameless man and, presumably, his wife. So I didn't think I was being the least bit impertinent when I said, "Now, Senator, won't you tell me your name?"

I'll never forget his horrified answer.

"Oh, *no*! I'm grateful to you, of course, but I can't afford to take the risk of any of my constituents finding out that I consulted a psychic. You understand. It's so . . . so . . . *flaky!*"

With that, the wire went dead.

Flaky! That senator was on my mind longer than he deserved to be after that phone clicked off. People like him and the constituents whose disapproval he feared prompted me to turn my back on any and all paranormal work for the next decade. The psychic waters I had chosen to explore had proven too turbulent. I fled back to the safer shores of ordinary existence.

4

Sensory Perception

ONE OF the friendships I most remember and cherish—and one that gave me some of my profoundest insights into the world beyond the five senses—was with the remarkably brilliant, multilingual Helen Keller. She was an emotional earthquake in my life, shaking me to my very soul.

When the play, *The Miracle Worker*, opened on Broadway in 1960, Dick and I went to see it and were profoundly moved. A year or so later, I took my daughter Jill to see it on her seventh birthday. She too was deeply touched by the electrifying story. Jill expressed a desire to meet Helen Keller, and I agreed that it would be a marvelous experience. My husband had a friend who knew her dedicated secretary, Evelyn Seide. Through her, we arranged a date for me to meet the great lady, who lived only ten minutes away from our home in Connecticut.

In preparation for our meeting, I studied the hand language that Miss Keller—who was deaf as well as blind—used to communicate. I also read the works of the Swedish religious teacher and mystic, Emmanuel Swedenborg, since I knew she was a Swedenborgian. I went alone on my first visit to Helen Keller, but after we became better acquainted, I asked if I could bring Jill to meet her. Miss Keller, who adored children, readily agreed.

Jill learned the hand language alphabet, and when she was introduced she slowly spelled out "How do you do, Miss Keller" in the gentle woman's palm.

Helen lightly touched the seven-year-old's dress and hair as she spelled out her introduction. Then she replied, in that unique, somewhat strained voice of hers, "How do you do, little dear. What

23

a beautiful blue dress you have on and what lovely red hair you have."

Jill was wide-eyed.

"How did she know that, Mommy?" she whispered.

"You don't have to whisper," I told her. "Miss Keller cannot hear or see you. She is very gifted and she uses her fingertips in place of her eyes."

"How does she do that?" Jill demanded.

The question gave me pause, and I remember struggling to find an answer for the bewildered child. "Well," I began, "there is normal perception through each of your five senses and there is *extra*sensory perception. . . ."

Jill waited for me to continue.

"Since Miss Keller has been deprived of her seeing and her hearing she has to use another way, some kind of extrasensory way, to do what she does. I don't know what it is exactly, but I'm going to find out, because I too would like to understand it."

The first step on the road to understanding what Helen Keller did was a thorough comprehension of how our usual five senses operate. I studied hard and, with the welcome help of several of my scientifically oriented friends, came up with an explanation that my seven-year-old could grasp. In the process of understanding normal sensory perception, NSP, for myself and for Jill, I was also building the bridge that would lead me into my work in extrasensory perception, ESP.

I learned that all sensory perception is the processing of certain waves or vibrations. Each of the senses is geared to monitor or receive these vibrations, very much like a radio receiver. When a vibration is received on the band of one of our five senses, it is converted into an electrical impulse in our neurological system and is then transmitted to the brain for interpretation. Since all sensory information is neutral, it is the interpretation of this information in the brain that describes what we see, hear, taste, smell, or touch. This is an overly simplified explanation, of course, but it enabled me to draw an analogy with which to explain the process to my small daughter.

"Jill, you know that we use our eyes for seeing, our ears for hearing, our noses for smelling, our tongues and the insides of our mouths for tasting, and our fingers and the other parts of our bodies for touching," I told her. "Each of our five senses is very much like a radio band, but on our sensory radio bands only certain signals can be picked up. When you tune into one of the frequencies you tune into seeing or hearing or tasting—"

Jill frowned in concentration for a few minutes, then she said, "But are there other signals that aren't on my sensory radio band?"

Pleased to see that she was getting the concept, I replied, "Yes, but your radio signal band can't pick them up. Think about the radio in your room. It has two bands, AM and FM. You can't listen to an FM station on your AM band, because it will not pick it up. The signal from the FM band is in your room ready to be received, but only if you turn on the FM button. Furthermore, once you lock into one band or station, all you can receive is information of one reality."

To further illustrate my point, I told Jill the famous story about the group of deaf people who sat through a concert, testified unanimously that they had not heard any music, and offered their experience as proof positive that music did not exist. She laughed and I continued: "The main thing to remember is that you may not be able to tune into a signal or vibration because you don't have the proper equipment, or because your equipment may not be in working order, but the signal is still there to be picked up. When the radio in your room is off, the signals that would make it play are still in your room. It's just that nothing is turned on to pick them up."

I still remember the excitement in Jill's voice as she grasped the analogy and asked, "Well, isn't that true for Helen Keller?"

"Good for you!" I exclaimed. "Even though two of her five sensory radio bands—seeing and hearing—do not work, the signals they would process if they *did* work are still there. Miss Keller has simply found another way to tune into them."

In the course of my friendship with Helen Keller, I discovered that when she attended concerts and plays, she "saw" and "heard" them by the vibrations they created. Helen's financial and personal secretary, Evelyn Seide, told me that Helen's fingers would twitch impatiently if the music was even slightly offbeat in the pieces she knew. After delivering a lecture of her own, Helen would determine the level of applause through vibrations in her feet. At the theater, she could follow the dialogue by placing her fingers on a section of the stage. Loving sculpture as she did, she explored its mystery through her fingertips.

Since the impulses conveyed to the brain through the various sensory pathways are always the same type, the numerous nerve endings at Helen's fingertips were able to pick up the vibrations normally reserved for the eyes and ears. When handed a rose, she could identify it as pink, yellow, red, or white, possibly through her sense of smell. It was really extraordinary, but I was not sure if it could truly be called extrasensory.

Helen *was* psychic, however; she had powers that went beyond her normal sensory perception. One afternoon she and I were sitting in her living room in Arcan Ridge, talking about a little ivory figure that had been given to her by the prime minister of India, Jawaharlal Nehru. "You must excuse me a moment, my dear," my hostess said unexpectedly, and just as suddenly slumped motionless in her chair.

I stared at her in bewilderment. About two minutes later, she again sat upright in her chair. "What happened?" I asked.

"I've been to the Alps," she replied calmly and proceeded to describe her visit to me for the next hour. There was no question in Helen's razor-sharp mind that she had actually been in the Alps. Her detailed descriptions indicated that a great deal more than the two minutes in my earth time frame had elapsed. She had had what is called an astral, or out-of-body, experience, she told me. It was then that I realized how very much I had to learn.

Before we can hope to understand ESP, we have to expand our knowledge of NSP. The evolution of higher forms of life was accompanied by the evolution of complex sense organs. Human beings normally operate with five senses. Each sense band picks up those frequencies or energy events or vibrations that occur within the limitations of the band. The infinitesimal waves that make up visible light, for example, are picked up by the eye. Our eyes, however, can barely register a single octave of the electromagnetic vibrations we call "light." This word *light* can also be quite correctly applied to the electromagnetic radiations on either side of the tiny band we can see with the naked eye.

The pressure waves vibrating in the air as sounds are picked up by the ears. I came to learn that the human ear can pick up about ten octaves of these acoustic waves and record them as sound. But there is also an unconscious perception of sound waves below the "normal range." Canadian scientist M. Persinger believes that many precognitive experiences result from this phenomenon.

The various bands detect and record all sorts of events around us—the drone of a bee on a summer day, the fragrant aroma of cookies baking, the biting wind as you ski down a high slope. These frequencies are then converted into electrical energy and transmitted to the brain in the form of nerve impulses. Science has known since the mid-nineteenth century that the nerve force is electrical.

As a result of the processing of electrical impulses in the central nervous system, we hear, taste, touch, smell, and see. The pulsings conveyed to the brain constitute the language of the nerve cells. Stimuli received through our five senses become our *experienced reality* or, as some people prefer to call it, our *objective reality*. It is all too easy for us to be unaware of our sense limitations and to classify all of our experiences within a "normal" range. And yet Helen Keller had given Jill and me proof positive that the radio bands on which we operate can be expanded. Deprived of both her audial and visual senses, Helen was nevertheless able to pick up the frequencies these two senses missed. She expanded her senses of taste, touch, and smell and was able to receive stimuli which are normally reserved for the eyes and ears. She had demonstrated that our sensory bands can be stretched to new limits. Why couldn't a person blessed with all of his five senses likewise expand his sensory bands and awareness?

Seeing Helen Keller in action, I couldn't help wondering if the development of a sixth sense to perceive new phenomena wasn't actually within the grasp of all of us.

My studies had taught me that the survival of any species depends on its ability to receive and translate the proper signals. Dogs have a sense of hearing that goes from 40 to 75 percent beyond the range of humans; their sense of smell is so keen they can detect the presence of other creatures in a particular area long after they've moved on. Every human being leaves a "scent print" as unique as his fingerprint. Salmon, using their olfactory sense, find their way back from the open sea, many thousands of miles, to the spawning grounds they left years before. Bats and tree shrews use an extended audial band to orient themselves to the world of darkness in which they live, and migrating songbirds are equipped with tiny sensors with which to check their flight patterns against the stars. Certain tropical fish travel unerringly through the rocks and shoals of muddy rivers by means of sensors that generate an electrical field that warns them of any obstacles in their path. All these uses of the senses by these creatures are perfectly "normal" for them.

As we know, white light breaks down into ten known colors of the spectrum. (There may even be more that have not yet been discovered.) We can see seven of these colors with our naked vision. The other three require special instruments to pick up their waves. Vipers, however, can see infrared and some insects see ultraviolet.

The marvelous geometrician, educator, architect-designer, and futuristic thinker, R. Buckminster Fuller, has said that "99 percent of the transactions of the Universe are ultra and infra to man's sensory tuning." He goes on to say that "*reality* is a broad spectrum of energy events across a small portion of which our senses can 'tune.' The Universe is the sum total of all experiences."

The world marveled at the way Helen Keller overcame her monumental handicaps and was able to live a normal and very productive life. She did it partly through her tremendous courage and willpower, but even more by developing alternative ways of sensing the vibrations that the rest of us pick up through seeing and hearing. In the process, she also developed the ability to tune into other vibrations that are not normal to any of the five human senses, the frequencies that might be called *ultra* or *infra*—above or below the human ranges of normal sensory awareness.

I have read that universal mind encompasses a limitless range of frequencies and continuous broadcasts. The more developed and perceptive an individual mind becomes, the greater the frequency range within universal mind that consciousness can tune in to.

Extrasensory perception is the expansion of our normal bands of perception to include frequencies or bands of information not found on our regular tuners. It is also the development of a "sixth" or intuitive sense. Helen Keller was able to do this. So do people who turn around when they feel someone staring at them from behind and find they are right. You do it when you pick up the telephone and say "hello" by name to the person on the other end of the line before he or she has spoken. Businessmen who get gut feelings or business hunches do it too, but too many of these so-called pragmatists prefer to label this instinct "judgment." And I do it, because I've worked long and hard to develop the ability to tune into the frequencies outside most people's normal ranges. My objective reality goes beyond ordinary sensory perceptions. A great many of the happenings, sights, and sounds that I've experienced on what I like to think of as my ultra high frequency or UHF band are far more subtle, and yet far more precise, than the things I have experienced with my five normal senses.

I learned a great deal from my friendship with Helen Keller, and my memories of that great lady are still very much alive. I was standing with Helen on her terrace one sunny day when she whistled softly. There was a rustling in the nearby treetops, and suddenly a dozen or more birds flew out of the branches and lighted on the terrace. One hopped right onto Helen's outstretched hand.

It was a charming and somewhat awesome sight, and I couldn't help sharing my reactions with Helen. "Oh, I wish my children could have seen you with those birds today," I tapped into her palm as I was saying goodbye.

On my next visit, Helen asked me to summon her gardener. "And tell him to bring in the surprise he made for you," she said.

The gardener appeared. I knew he had constructed the assortment of beautiful birdhouses and feeders that dotted Helen's property. Now he was carrying two more birdhouses—one an "apartment building" for martins, the other, a tiny wren house.

My eyes filled with tears as Helen gently murmured, "For you and the children, my dear, so that you can see and hear the birds that I cannot."

Those lovely birdhouses still hang in our trees. The large one is in a clump of birch by the terrace, and the wren house perches in a handsome old oak. We have enjoyed watching and listening to our martins and wrens for well over a decade, but I never do so without recalling Helen Keller, who, in spite of being blind and deaf, could— in her own way—see and hear them too.

5

The Good Doctor

IN THE MID-1960s I decided to turn my
back on the world of ESP. I had done so once before, unconsciously,
when, as a child, I grew tired of being told that I had a vivid imagination. Now it was a conscious decision. As an adult I felt that
I was too often at the mercy of people who did not understand or
respect any kind of psychic ability.

At the time I thought my withdrawal would be permanent;
it was another decade before I found that I was wrong. On the
morning of March 6, 1976, three of my children and I were gathered
at Emerson College in Boston to watch my husband Dick receive an
honorary degree. He was made a Doctor of Laws *honoris causa* for
his work in "bringing to educational institutions the practical wisdom of the marketplace and a wide knowledge of men and affairs."

As we sat there listening to this citation with tears of pride in
our eyes, none of us could have known how much that occasion would
change our lives. We did not realize that as we were happily welcoming one distinguished and deserving doctor into our family, we were
also on the verge of welcoming another doctor—the one we would
come to call the "Good Doctor"—into our lives.

On this particular trip to Boston, Dick and I had taken a suite
instead of our usual room at the Ritz-Carlton Hotel. I had arranged
to interview some candidates for one of my executive search firm
clients while we were there. With such spacious quarters at our
disposal, we decided to invite the president of Emerson College, Dr.
Gus Turbeville, and his wife to join us for the evening. Dr. Turbeville asked if he could bring along a guest, a gentleman who was

visiting the campus and was eager to meet me—Dr. Andrija Puharich.

The name was more than familiar to me, and I was both pleased and flattered at the prospect of meeting this eminent man. An M.D. as well as an honorary LL.D., Dr. Puharich had done extensive work with the deaf, patenting more than sixty devices in phono reception. In the 1950s he had made one of the earliest and most extensive investigations of psychedelic substances, resulting in the publication of his trailblazing book, *The Sacred Mushroom*.

Dr. Puharich had also done a great deal of writing and lecturing in the field of psi research and was reputed to be one of the world's foremost authorities on parapsychology.

Gus Turbeville had visited us some months before, and noticed that our library contained an extensive collection of books on extrasensory perception. That, plus his recollection of several intuitive remarks I had made about him, had prompted Emerson's president to mention me to Dr. Puharich. What Dr. Turbeville did not know, however, was that I had been actively psychic some years before we met. Nor was he aware that I had deliberately dropped all psychic activity from my life.

I was far more excited at the thought of meeting Dr. Puharich than he could possibly have been about meeting me. He was a rather famous person, while I had remained anonymous during my own limited participation in the field.

On that March evening in Boston, the Turbevilles and Dr. Puharich came to our suite accompanied by several of Emerson's trustees and a number of faculty members. I was soon speaking with Dr. Puharich, and it didn't take long for him to suggest that we retreat to one of the unoccupied rooms in the suite and try an experiment in hypnosis. I was hesitant at first, and begged off, claiming that I had to see to our guests. It was not a very good excuse. Everyone was relaxed and sociable; there was really no need for me to stay.

Sensing my hesitance, Dr. Puharich tactfully invited one of the trustee's wives to join us in the other room. To further divert my attention from the impending hypnotism, he asked me to try and "pick up some impressions" of the woman. I had met her casually and exchanged a few polite words of conversation with her earlier in the day. But I knew little about her except her name. However,

I agreed to give her a reading by psychometrizing her watch, just as Mary had done with my own watch fifteen years before.

The images came rapidly and I couldn't stop talking. Before long, I was touching on some pressing and highly personal problems and the woman begged me to stop. She seemed to be greatly disturbed by what I had picked up. Overcome with emotion, she wiped her eyes, squeezed my hand, and fled from the room.

Although I had warned Andrija Puharich that I didn't think I would be a very good hypnotic subject, my ability at psychometry persuaded him otherwise. I remember nothing of the incident beyond removing my shoes and belt, stretching out on the bed, and listening to Dr. Puharich's persuasive voice counting . . . counting . . . counting. . . .

Apparently we met with success beyond the Good Doctor's expectations, for when I sat up at the close of the session, there were tears of excitement in his eyes. The first words he spoke after the hypnosis were, "My dear child, through you I have been speaking in Arabic to an old friend of mine. He was Eileen Garrett's guide and he always greeted me in a very private way known only to us both."

Dr. Puharich had run an investigative group, The Roundtable, in Maine during the late 1940s, and Eileen Garrett had been one of its members. The Irish-born clairvoyant was unquestionably one of the most remarkable psychics of the twentieth century. I knew all about the voices from other lands and times who regularly spoke through her. Now one of them had evidently spoken through me. It was hard to believe.

"In Arabic? Me? Impossible!" I blurted out.

This was to be the first of many such sessions with Dr. Puharich. At the time, we had no way of knowing where our adventure would lead. Who could have dreamed that it would span time and space and planets and galaxies and dimensions and, in truth, propel us to the realm of extraterrestrial intelligence?

Dr. Puharich was anxious to continue working with me, and by now I was too intrigued to do anything but agree. Both of us led busy lives, so it was some time before we could begin our work. It was not until the following November that my family and I saw him again. The date was November 27, 1976. I invited him to our home for Thanksgiving dinner, and we settled down in the living room to an amazing conversation. Or perhaps I should call it a monologue, since the Good Doctor left the rest of us speechless.

Andrija (which he insisted we call him) put everyone at ease with his naturally warm manner. He drew out our four children on their feelings about extrasensory matters and found them all surprisingly well informed and sympathetic to the subject. None of them was unduly skeptical, but they were far from gullible either.

The Good Doctor found out that the youngsters had always been strongly supportive of my interest in the paranormal and frequently encouraged me to get back into psychic activity. Andrija commented on what intelligent children we had and was delighted with our shared interest and curiosity about psi phenomena.

If there was one man on the face of the globe qualified to satisfy that curiosity, it was Andrija. When he started discussing his work in psi research, he fascinated, captivated, and tantalized us all. His current project, he told us, was lining up a group of thirty-six people—he called them "Space Kids"—to participate in a special experiment he planned for the end of August.

Naturally we wanted to know what the experiment was and how he was going to select his thirty-six subjects. He explained that he had already investigated hundreds of people under scientific conditions at Lab Nine, his headquarters in Ossining, New York. His aim was to determine if any of them had what I later came to call "cosmic connections" to other dimensionalities.

A major portion of Andrija's group had already been found. Some were high-wired for particular information in nuclear physics beyond what scientists have unlocked so far. Some were catalysts to keep others on a direct course. Some were telepathic. Some had unusual musical and linguistic gifts.

Although Andrija's dubbing of his subjects as Space Kids suggested a certain frivolity, one thing was unfrivolously clear: he was firmly convinced that he had developed a foolproof laboratory technique for pinpointing certain people who had the ability to return to a "parent civilization" and awaken to their purpose or "mission" on Earth.

We listened to Andrija's stories of these Space Kids with some reservations and a certain amount of skepticism. He then proceeded to tell us his scenario for what he "knew" to be the future of Planet Earth.

In brief, he said that in the coming decade we would have a series of drastic shifts in land masses. Havoc would be wrought by volcanoes, earthquakes, tidal waves, famine, disease. Land would appear and disappear, and close to 40 percent of the world's population would be decimated through nature's destruction—the Earth's natural processes for cleansing itself—and through our own inability to cope with the massive changes.

We were thunderstruck by what we were hearing. It boggled our minds and staggered our imaginations. In a calm, detached fashion, Andrija was telling us that close to 2 billion people were going to die in a decade. A "New Age" was on its way, he insisted. As this man-for-all-seasons quietly narrated his scenario of destruction and reconstruction, the six of us sat alternately horrified, fascinated, dubious—and yet respectful.

But why was he telling us all this? And why did he persist in declaring that I could contribute to his work?

I soon had the answers to both my questions. In his gentle, understated manner, Andrija indicated his desire to have me visit Lab Nine and undergo the procedure he used for selecting his Space Kids. He needed only a few more people to round out his thirty-six, and he was hoping I might be one of the subjects he sought.

I laughed at the idea, but my family did not find it the least bit amusing. Why not? they demanded. What did I have to lose? Even though I had refused to acknowledge my psychic abilities in recent years, there was no question that I was gifted. Besides, this was a unique project. I wouldn't have to participate in any further research if I didn't want to; but the testing experience itself would be fascinating, wouldn't it?

If I was worried about looking foolish, that too could be solved. I didn't have to tell anyone about the experiment, and Andrija, too, would protect my anonymity. My husband, my four children, and Andrija kept trying to persuade me all through our Thanksgiving dinner and on into the evening. I felt my self-protective armor weakening before this assault on all sides by so many bright and verbal people. Before Andrija said good night, I had agreed to think about his suggestion.

My head was swimming when I fell into bed that night. I had seen the gleam of excited anticipation in the eyes of my husband and children. They had all told me they trusted Andrija and felt that under his expert guidance I had nothing to fear, nothing to lose— and possibly something wondrous to gain. As I closed my eyes, I remember remarking to Dick that I was sure I wouldn't sleep a wink. When morning arrived, I found that I had slept so soundly that I barely rumpled the sheets.

At breakfast, everyone was anxiously waiting to hear my decision. I told them that I was eager to establish a credible basis for the holocaustic picture Andrija had painted. I could not subscribe to such a devastating idea without some further confirmation of his theory from documented reliable sources. Dick and our children agreed. They were as unwilling as I was to accept such predictions from only one source.

I strongly sensed that there was a connection between the scenario Andrija had so graphically spun and his search for Space Kids. But that was not my only reason for accepting his invitation to be tested at Lab Nine. I realized that if anyone was ever going to study my psychic abilities, Dr. Andrija Puharich was the best-qualified person to do it. If I was going to reenter the psychic world, he was the one person who could lead me. His experience and credentials would give my efforts the support and credibility they had lacked when I had worked alone in the past.

Andrija called the next evening to thank us for our hospitality. He paid us a number of compliments on our family, and couldn't stop marveling at the serenity and solidarity of our home life. Eventually he came to the crucial question: had I slept on my decision to come work with him?

I said yes, but I warned him that my business schedule was always extremely crowded at the end of the year. On the other hand, I confessed that it tickled me to think of embarking on this new adventure on or around my forty-sixth birthday. We got out our calendars and managed to work out a mutually agreeable date for December 17, the day after my birthday.

Andrija had promised over Thanksgiving dinner that Dick could be at my side while I submitted to his tests and that he could even enter the copper Faraday Cage where the hypnosis sessions would be conducted. I reminded the Good Doctor of that promise now. Andrija said that he had never before allowed anyone to enter his copper room except the subjects he was working with, but he agreed once more to make exception for Dick. He also reiterated his promise to guarantee my privacy and had no objection to my request that Dick be allowed to join him in recording and transcribing the proceedings.

As I hung up the phone after Andrija's call, I felt a curious mixture of hesitation and relief. I had long known that I had psychic abilities, but I had always told myself that if I could do extraordinary things, there couldn't be any great mystery to it. In Aristotelian logic this is called syllogistic reasoning, i.e.:

I have extrasensory perception.

I am not mysterious.

Therefore, ESP is not mysterious!

Yet ten years after abandoning my psychic research, I was still somewhat mystified by psychic phenomena. I wanted and needed the advice, confirmation, and encouragement of an expert.

Have you ever heard that old adage, "When the student is ready, the teacher appears"?

I knew now that I was finally ready, and miraculously my teacher had appeared.

6

A Wondrous Entity

DECEMBER 17, the day we were scheduled to start working with Andrija, turned out to be a raw, windy day. I had a heavy chest cold, and I fretted all the way to Ossining, because I was convinced that I'd be unable to summon up any psychic energy for this first Lab Nine meeting. The common cold dulls the normal five senses, so there was no doubt in my mind that the extrasensory and paranormal abilities would also be blunted.

When we arrived at the main house of the Puharich compound, Andrija greeted us warmly, but I was distressed to find that the house was extremely chilly. A lighting fixture had just short-circuited, Andrija explained, and he had opened all the windows to let out the acrid smell. Huddled in the living room in my fleece-lined coat, I began to articulate my misgivings about the undertaking. Andrija listened politely but unsympathetically.

"You were pretty reluctant to be hypnotized when we first met in Boston," he reminded me. "You were sure you wouldn't be a good subject."

I laughed, remembering my trepidation.

Now, nine months after our first meeting and three weeks after our second, we sat in Andrija's living room and got reacquainted—psychically. Andrija started off just as he had in Boston by asking me to pick up any impressions that came to mind. I immediately asked, "Who is Marilyn?"

The answer: one of his Space Kids who had left the lab a few hours before.

"I also sense something personal about the word *tickled*, or is it *ticklish*? Does tickling have some special meaning for you?"

Again I was right on target. Andrija's late wife had been extremely ticklish. He and Julie, another Space Kid, had discussed it earlier in the day.

Another word popped into my consciousness: *"Triangle,* no, that's *triad.* What does it mean?"

Andrija was working on a special project with a woman from Israel and a man from England. They referred to themselves as the Triad.

Two of my impressions that afternoon had no meaning at the time: the word *Astri* and name *Shames.* But I scored about a dozen other hits and Andrija, rubbing his hands in satisfaction, announced that we had to go ahead with our experiment. "You are clicking beautifully, despite your cold," he said.

The Good Doctor led us through his spacious house, stopping en route to show us his Faraday Cage, a room constructed completely of copper so that—with the possible exception of extra-low-frequency waves, known as ELF—no sound or object could penetrate its thick walls.

The room contained some recording equipment and several sophisticated electronic devices that Andrija had invented for his auditory work. There were, in addition, three straight-backed chairs, some tables, special shelves to hold the equipment, and a collection of quilts on the floor. Although the room reminded me of some kind of copper meat locker, I knew that Andrija had performed some notable experiments in the previous Faraday Cage he had set up during the days of his famous Roundtable in Maine.

We were whisked upstairs to another working space. Technically Andrija's bedroom, it was equipped with complex recording devices and lined with floor-to-ceiling bookshelves. The volumes they contained reflected the amazing scope of this man's research interests. A globe showing the stars and constellations was on the raised desk, and a king-sized bed flanked one wall. The room was decorated with some fascinating prints and paintings along with some photographs that Andrija had taken of UFOs. Some interesting bits and pieces of bent metal, spoons, sculpture, and odd coins were artfully arranged on several of the shelves.

The room was warm and pleasant, and I promptly announced that I'd rather stay right there than go back downstairs to the copper cage. Andrija was agreeable. He set up his equipment while I stretched out on the bed, and Dick settled beside us on the floor with his tape recorder ready to spin.

I don't feel that I have the right to reveal the details of Andrija's carefully developed technique for locating his Space Kids. But I will outline the general procedure that he used to bring me to an altered state of consciousness. He started the session by putting me into a light stage of hypnosis, much as he had done at our initial meeting in Boston. Being a trusting, willing, and conditioned subject, I made his task as easy as I could, even though I wasn't feeling my best. It takes quite a bit of self-discipline to be able to screen out noises, voices, random thoughts from the mind. The ego and the willpower must be silenced. The gatekeeper of the conscious mind is one's will.

The main problem, however, is fear, on a conscious or subconscious level. Fear of the unknown, fear of a lack of control of one's actions, fear of the concept and possible consequences. Having complete faith in Andrija and my environment and knowing that my husband was at my side, I was able to relax and cooperate fully. I listened and followed the gentle voice counting . . . counting . . . "ten, nine, eight— Relax. Breathe deeply." The voice faded into nothingness. I was "under" but aware, very aware, of the doctor's voice.

Andrija and I shared a magnificent sight which Dick was unable to see: a golden burst of starlike dots blanketing the ceiling. It looked like a comet made of millions of tiny gold stars with shimmering clusters that were especially bright on the right side. I had the feeling I was floating, and I had no sense of time. Time dilation is not detectable sensorily. We measure time in a manner unique to the needs of Planet Earth, but not to the needs of the rest of the Universe. As Andrija carried me into a deeper hypnotic state, I was prepared to get out of my body: to travel astrally.

The idea of an out-of-body experience was not strange to me. I had observed Helen Keller take a two-minute trip to the Alps and realized as she recounted the story that it transcended minutes and all other human time-frame references. I had, in addition, read any number of books that told of the out-of-body experiences of people from all walks of life and many parts of the world. Some of the literature described the entities they had encountered in their discarnate travels. It was not unheard of, for example, for a person thousands of miles away to appear and bid a last farewell to a loved one before dying in some far-off place.

I was prepared for many of the possibilities that an astral trip might bring and agreed with E. F. Schumacher's statement, "Man is *capax universi*—capable of bringing the whole universe into his experience." But I was not ready for an experience of such proportions that it made the objective reality of my early experience seem inadequate and impoverished.

More than four years later I still remember that first session vividly, as I came face to face with a tunnel and a wondrous entity with unforgettable eyes. Dick's tapes provide accuracy that memory cannot. In the following transcript, A is Andrija, G is Greta.

A: Describe him to me, please.

G: He's got the most marvelous eyes—golden, human, marvelous eyes. His upper lip is sort of birdlike, but he has very human eyes.

A: Try to speak to him. Where is he from?

G: I see two others exactly like the first one.

A: Try to speak to them. One will step forward and act as spokesman.

G: One is contacting me, but his lips don't move.

A: They communicate telepathically. What does he say?

G: His name is Shames. They are sent from Ogatta. Does that ring a bell?

A: Do they have a message for me?

G: I am so near the tunnel.

A: Try to get through that tunnel. There will be light on the other side.

G: I'm trying. . . . I can't seem to get through.

A: Keep trying.

G: Yes. But those birdlike men are in the tunnel. They are guarding it and I cannot get through there. I see a structure. There is a fence around it.

A: Try to go inside.

G: I can't find the opening.

A: There has to be an opening. Keep looking.

G: I'm trying but I can't . . . I can't. . . . He wants to tell me something. His lips don't move but I understand him! What wonderful eyes! He says he is from Mennon, many light-ages away, and that I am from Ogatta, many light-ages away. Oh, when he looks into my eyes it's unbelievably beautiful . . . beautiful.

A: Yes.

G: I cannot go through the tunnel yet. Ssshh! He is looking into my eyes.

Dick's notes record that at that point I suddenly sighed deeply and a basso voice coming out of my throat said, "Energy level low on the bed." I then stirred, and in a normal voice asked if a child were crying.

A: Yes. Sorry for the disturbance. There is a child crying out in the hall. We'll stop, and I'll bring you out properly now.

Andrija aborted the session after one hour and some minutes. He was terribly excited about my prospects and confided that no one had ever gone so far as to have their "parent civilization" revealed to them in a first session. He was further impressed because we were not even in the copper cage. He urged me to get well and set aside a four-day period to work day and night with him. Dick would be right there as promised, and since I had no memory of what happened during the session, I could listen, as I did that evening, to his tapes of the proceedings.

Andrija stressed the desirability of working in his soundproof copper cage the next time we met. He was also extremely positive and excited about my future prospects. We left Lab Nine with a sense of urgency and burgeoning curiosity. What would transpire once we really got down to work?

Dick and I discussed the session in great detail as we drove home . that evening. We both marveled at how little relevancy time and distance had when it came to traveling through the Cosmos. Shames had claimed to have come to us from a place that was "many light-ages away." Andrija had reminded us that a single light-age was 100,000 million light-years. One light-year was 5 trillion, 875 billion miles. I didn't even know how many zeros were involved in that figure.

Dick and I discussed the fact that all of us are basically pragmatic. We accept the odds and probabilities that life deals out. We have been conditioned by baseball averages, political polls, census takers, income tax tables, life expectancy charts. All of us are aware that the average American family has 2.3 children and that the odds of winning the Irish Sweepstakes are over 500,000 to one. But how would the average person react to Shames's estimate of Ogatta's distance from Earth?

"Well," Dick said with a grin, "how would people react to finding life in the Cosmos if they were familiar with the statistics our astronomers are working with today?"

That was a fair point. Do you know the statistics? They're stranger than science fiction!

Astronomers calculate that our galaxy, the Milky Way, has approximately *100 billion* stars in it besides our Sun. To the best of our current knowledge, the Universe is composed of *100 billion galaxies,* each consisting of an estimated *100 billion stars* within the galaxies. If we took all of the stars in all of the galaxies and were to put a number down on paper, it would be *10 billion trillion* (10^{22}) stars! Our own star, the Sun, is thought to be a second- or even third-generation star, made from matter produced in the interior of a giant red star that died over 5 billion years ago. Imagine, in a geological time frame a star has a birth, life, and death, just as we do.

Dr. Carl Sagan, professor of astronomy and space sciences at Cornell University, states that both theory and observation now suggest that planets are a common, if not invariable, accompaniment of stars, rather than an exceedingly rare occurrence, as was commonly believed in the first decade of this century. If this is the case, how difficult is it to imagine a solar system circling a star 1 billion years older than our Sun? The inhabitants, if there are any, would be a billion years more advanced than ourselves. Now, a billion years in the process of evolution is a long time. On the Earth, the most advanced form of life a billion years ago was the earthworm! Could the inhabitants of an older solar system be as different from us as we, the human species, are from the earthworm?

With these statistics and conjectures as a base, and believing that we have not yet discovered all of the bodies in our own solar system (let alone within other systems that might orbit other stars in the Milky Way or other galaxies), can pragmatism refute the existence of life on a planet other than Earth? As Dr. Lewis Thomas, president of Memorial Sloan-Kettering Cancer Center, puts it, "We live in a very small spot, and for all we know there may be millions of other small spots like ours in the millions of other galaxies: in theory, the universe can sprout life any old time it feels like it." A year or so was to pass before one of the Ogatta group commented that in our lifetime we would see another planet in our solar system and advised us that there are still others of which we will not be aware for many more years.

We turned into our driveway and I emitted an enormous sneeze. Dick and I both laughed. I might be able to consort with beings from other dimensions, but I still couldn't shake the common cold!

7

On Being a Channel

I HAD DISLIKED being referred to as a medium or a psychic during my active work in the paranormal. Now I was being labeled a channel. This was the word Andrija used to describe what had happened in our session.

According to the Good Doctor, that first session in Boston—when someone named Abdul had spoken through me in Arabic—clearly indicated that I was a channel. Hearing him describe that basso-profundo voice speaking through me had been vastly unsettling. I was equally taken aback at our next session to hear the voice of Shames speaking to Andrija through my vocal chords. This was particularly startling since Shames talked to *me* telepathically, not moving his lips but linking into my thoughts with his large, luminous, gold-flecked eyes.

I didn't mind *being* a channel, but I disliked being called one. One of the major problems with words, I find, is that they limit our ability to think. We tend to become too bound up in them. Language simply is not an adequate standard against which *thinking* should be measured. Too many concepts get lost in the tangle of words. As Tauri, my most faithful visitor from the Ogatta group, says so often, "Look not to the quantity of words, but to the quality of thoughts. The quality of the thought is the soul of the idea."

Anyone who has ever felt something deep in his soul, but was unable to explain either the sensation or the reason for it, knows this frustration well. For the present, however, words are the sole means we have of communicating on a broad scale. But the time will come, I assure you, when we will all be able to communicate telepathically.

Chuang Tsu, the Taoist Chinese philosopher, recognized the problem: "The rabbit snare exists because of the rabbit. Once you've

44

got the rabbit, you can forget the snare. Words exist because of the meaning. Once you've gotten the meaning, you can forget the words. Where can I find a man who has forgotten the words so I can have a word with him?"

Just think about some of the words those in the psychic community are stuck with: aura, trance, materialization, dematerialization, UFO, psychometry, telepathy, teleportation, psychic surgery, ETI, etc. These words sound odd to me, and I cringe when I'm forced to use them to describe an experience or thought. Even the words "parapsychology" and "paranormal" set my teeth on edge, because I am convinced from both personal experience and scientific evidence that "paranormal" processes are *not* "beyond" or "aside from" reality —they are very much a part of reality.

The scientific community has a standard set of words to describe various phenomena, but the psychic community is so disorganized and disparate that it cannot even agree on its terms. Be that as it may, whether I liked it or not, I was stuck with being labeled a channel—not exactly a household word for anyone not familiar with the psychic field. What exactly is a channel?

The dictionary defines it as follows. *Channel, noun*: The mechanism providing a single path in multipath systems for simultaneously and separately recording or transmitting sounds from more than one source. *Channel, verb*: To direct through or into a direct course.

My own definition carries this idea a step further. *Channel, noun*: A human being through whom things happen and information is transmitted in an awakened or a sleeping state; a human whose body is used by other beings for the purpose of disseminating technical and/or nontechnical data. *Channel, verb*: to provide the facility through which another being can communicate.

The concept of what a channel is can be clarified in what I call my "automobile analogy." Visualize three identical cars that have just come off the assembly line, waiting to be driven away. All three have the same components in their chassis, but will they all have the same life span, measured in miles driven? The odds are certainly against it. One car might go 125,000 miles, another 80,000 and the third perhaps only 40,000 or so. If they are identical cars, made on the same assembly line with all the same parts, why should this be so? (I can't answer the question, but I do know that it happens to all sorts of things, including human beings. Just look at the disparity of our life spans!)

Now let's suppose that we put drivers of differing abilities into the three identical cars. One is a professional race car driver, who can make his car perform in a manner the other two drivers cannot. The second is the average man or woman behind the wheel; the third is a terrible driver who probably shouldn't be allowed out on the roads or highways at all. Will it matter which car each of these drivers takes?

Not a bit! The professional racer will outperform the other two whether he is behind the wheel of the 125,000-mile car or the 40,000-mile car. Similarly, the average driver will continue to be average, and the poor driver will go on being a menace on the highways.

This situation is reflected in the performances of human beings in other areas as well. Our accomplishments are not predicated on how long we live—just as the drivers' abilities do not correspond to the life spans of their cars—but depend instead on what we do in the length of time allotted to us.

A classic example of this is the great composer, Wolfgang Amadeus Mozart. He started composing at the age of five and completed no less than 600 musical works—operas, sonatas, concertos, and symphonies (forty-one of them!)—before his death at the age of thirty-five.

In the next step of my automobile analogy, we fuse the driver with the car to form a mirror image of a human being. The soul (or driver) joins the body (or car) at the instant of birth. For all practical purposes, the body and soul (the car and driver) are one and the same. Indivisible. But, suppose the driver were able to get *out* of his car and let another driver get behind the wheel. Or suppose the driver were able to slide over into the passenger seat and let another driver pilot the car.

Or to look at my analogy from the flip side: suppose the soul were to get out of the one body and let another soul come in and use the body. Or, suppose the soul were able to move over but not leave the body while this other soul was in the body. Think about the separation of the functions of body/automobile from the functions of driver/soul. Human beings are not accustomed to thinking this way, but this is exactly what happens when a person acts as a channel. This is what I do.

Being a channel means moving out of your body or moving over in your body and letting another being use the physical vehicle. In the early stages of being a channel, I used to move or be moved out of my body to make way for another driver. Now, I can also slide over into the passenger seat and share the experience with the other driver. In short, a channel can drive his or her own car, or he can move over and share the driving with another driver. Or he can leave the car and let someone else drive it—or guard it—in his absence.

This automobile analogy is also useful for anyone who is trying to make sense out of reincarnation—a theory that most Easterners accept and most Westerners reject summarily. At the end of your car's allotted mileage, when it is ready to be hauled off to the junkyard, would you consider being hauled off with it? I doubt it.

As attached as some of us become to our automobiles, none of us would think of being buried with them. No. We say goodbye to our old cars and continue life without them. It is the same way with human life. When the body dies, the soul departs, but it continues to exist on its own. There have been quite a number of cases in which people were pronounced dead but were subsequently revived, literally brought back to life. In every instance, they reported being separated from their bodies as they watched their own deaths. They can also describe in minute detail the efforts made by doctors and nurses to save them. Many can repeat verbatim the conversations held by the medical teams who were working to keep them alive. Dr. Elisabeth Kübler-Ross, Col. Arthur E. Powell, and Dr. Raymond Moody are among the long list of medical and scientific experts who have written books on this subject, documenting their accounts with actual hospital records.

Separation of car and driver? Body and soul? The analogy is fascinating to contemplate.

Much as I complain about being labeled a channel, I cannot deny that I am one. This was not always the case. Or to be more accurate, let me say that I did not always *know how to use my ability* as a channel.

But then again, I didn't always know how to drive a car either.

8

Glancing Upward

TWO WEEKS passed before Dick and I could schedule four days to work around the clock with Andrija. While our businesses would suffer, we felt it was imperative that we continue the sessions in the copper cage and try to learn as much about the place called Ogatta as possible. The thought of a "parent civilization" in another galaxy was a lot to swallow.

We arrived at Lab Nine and almost the first statement out of my mouth was: "Who is Chris?" Andrija smiled. "Oh, what a great beginning!" he said. "Chris is a fifteen-year-old who arrived only a few minutes before you did. He's upstairs now. It's terrific that you pick up these things the way you do."

We went into the copper room, and I watched Dick and the doctor set up their recording equipment. Then I flopped onto the floor where the quilts were piled, kicked off my shoes, loosened my waistband, and got the feeling of the shiny, quiet space. Once the doors were closed and bolted, and the regular lights turned off, everyone could clearly see the digital clock with its numbers clicking away. A very dim, blue light which afforded no glare or distraction glowed overhead. Dick tucked quilts around me and moved to one side of the room. Andrija sat right behind me, so that when I looked up, his head was peering over mine, electronic equipment dangling from his ears.

I felt very safe within the cage's walls and I dreamily thought about the people who wear copper rings and bracelets for good health, good luck, and an assortment of other reasons. Settling down, I listened to Andrija record the time and date on his tape. The countdown and countback began in the first of what were to be about a dozen sessions which invariably ended in exactly one hour. Once I was in a hypnotic or trance state, my eyes were closed so I could not see the clock, but I seemed to have a timer all my own. What I did *not* have was a background in science or mathematics. I mention this because much of what was to ensue included the channeling of scientific data and mathematical formulae which made sense to the physicists and scientists who reviewed it, but not to me.

In the first session I had met Shames, whose name you will recall I had picked out of the air when I first entered Andrija's living room on December 17. This time HSHAMES came through and spelled his name properly for Dick to transcribe. He also corrected the spelling of the other word I had picked up: it was Astrae not Astri. We were told that Astrae was a minor Planet that Andrija should investigate via "the Berlin Maps." This was for purposes known only to the Good Doctor. (It was Hshames who first called him that.) Hshames also mentioned "Vesta" but said little about it. We would later make a connection between Astrae and Vesta when we learned that Vesta is the fourth minor Planet of the 1,700 already numbered Planets in the asteroid belt. We quickly discovered that everything ever channeled by the ETI had a connection to other channeled information.

Once the preliminaries were behind us, I found myself gazing once again into the eyes of Hshames. Big, wonderful, gold-flecked eyes they were, lashless, but hugely human in a face strangely bird-like. While Dick and Andrija could not see Hshames, I could not hear him when he used my body to speak with them. It was a real shock to hear Hshames's rich, deep voice on both tapes. When Hshames addressed *me*, it was telepathically. I immediately "linked into" the eyes and discovered in so doing that telepathizing with this entity was quite natural. I stared long and hard at him. He was not as tall as I am (I stand over five feet seven inches), and the fact that he did not have skin like mine did not startle me until I was back in my own body.

At first I had misgivings about getting out of my body. I was told by the Good Doctor again and again that he would protect my physical form carefully and I should never fear being unable to return to it. It seems strange that I should have worried, for once I finally reached Ogatta, I had no desire to come back to the middle-aged vehicle I could clearly see lying on the quilts on the floor of the cage. Later—much later—I learned from my husband that when I went out of my body for the first time, he had asked Andrija what would happen if I did not return. "She would stay out there and her body would die," Andrija had answered very softly. "She would die as we know death. Not to worry, though . . ." (Dick worried!)

Once again I came face to face with the tunnel. I knew that I had to get through it before I could reach my destination, whatever and wherever it might be. As in the first session, however, I could not get through. When I finally made it, during the third cage session, I was in a place where everyone welcomed me and recognized me. I was called "Plura" and I was on Ogatta.

While my earthly body lay in Ossining, New York, in a sound trance-state or deep sleep, my soul was on Ogatta in an altered state of consciousness. My physical vehicle operated on "automatic pilot," devoid of any sensation. My memories of this initial trip are extremely vivid on certain points, and nonexistent on others. The Ogatta experience I recall 100 percent; it's an experience I will treasure for the rest of my life on Earth. But more than a year elapsed before I could remember in my waking state anything else about my dealings with those beautiful extraterrestrial beings. I would listen to Dick and Andrija talk for hours about the sessions, as they would play and replay the tapes. I myself had no recollection of anything that transpired during the hours that I was on the floor of the cage.

At 11:09 A.M., on December 30, an entity named Ogatta channeled through me and for the first of only two occasions spoke with Andrija and Dick. Part of the transcript follows. Since this is straight channeling, I will not refer to myself as G for Greta unless I am *consciously* speaking myself. I shall refer to the entities by initials: O for Ogatta, H for Hshames, etc. Andrija will be AP and Dick will be D.

AP: I hear you perfectly, and Dick and I are standing by and guarding the body. Please explain why you called Greta by the name Plura?

O: Greta is on your planet as woman, but an atom can split from itself. Here she is Plura. As you call it . . . a fission. She does her jobs at two levels of simultaneous existence. As the atom divides itself, so can divide the personality. Do you understand that completely? It is important that all of you do. Souls can go to more than one planet at a time. Is that clear to you?

AP: Most definitely. I have known this to be the truth with others.

o: Good. Plura is an entity unto herself as is Greta. Greta has a job to do. A "mission" to accomplish. She knows her mission.

AP: Yes, yes! We want to know what that is. She has to remember. Before you take her could you tell me please if you talk to her telepathically on Ogatta?

o: If she but knew it, she will link all the telepathic energies we need to make communication possible. Soon you will talk to Tauri who will prefer to manifest as a child. Do not let her fool you! She has the wisdom of the ages. She is on Vesta in your own solar system but she is from Ogatta. Ask her what you will, and enjoy her visits to you.

AP: Vesta . . . Greta mentioned Vesta. Someone named Hshames mentioned it.

o: Hshames is from Mennon but he is on Vesta now too. It exists as a way station for us to use to help your planet. Time . . . out there . . . is not as you recognize it, but not that far distant. Just into the next dimensionality. Tauri will talk to you through Greta, but *to* Greta she can link telepathically as can we all. But for the reasons Greta is on Earth—

AP: Yes! Tell us if you will so that we can help her fulfill the mission.

o: She chose to come. She knew she had to establish a strong credibility through her family—husband and children—and through her work. The first three steps are behind her. The fourth stage was to return here which she has done, thanks to you. And now, we come to the crux of the matter. There is a coming in these decades, and she has a job to do. Will she *trumpet the voice and move the pen* as she must do? That is the question. That is the job. Many experiences, "lifetimes" if you will, went into the makings for her. She is not to write of past lifetimes and this is why she will have a block of memory of her past endeavors. Others will have full memory, she will have none, and they must not concern her or you. Do you understand so far?

AP: I do. She is to write and speak out on what subjects, Ogatta?

o: First, I take her by the hand and she will know. She will know me. Please stand by. [*Long pause.*]
She knows. There is a gathering together from many civilizations who will help your planet, Earth. They will come in craft we call the gattae. The way station is on Vesta, and you will hear more about that at another time. This child is to speak out on the coming of the gattae. She knows her mission, as you call it. And, another

phase already accomplished for you, in finding one more of your—
why do you call them—space children? She must do what she
agreed to do. I will tell you how to help her.

AP: Please. Give us the recipe.

O: You will work closely together, and she will stay under your um-
brella for a year, and then she must . . . she must step from behind
the comforting shadow. She has a year to prepare to trumpet the
voice and scribe the pen.

AP: Will she practice psychic things? Will she continue to do healings
and will she do occasional teleportation or materializations?

O: She wanted to be able to *see*. You call it clairvoyance. She wanted
to be able to *hear*. Clairaudience. She is, however, clairsensient.
She has the ability as no other to "sense," for she must sharpen
herself to communicate telepathically. She has glimpses of "seeing"
and "hearing," but it is the telepathy she must develop. Richard
knows some part of what she can do. We did some experiments
with her. She herself does not know all that she can do. That she
must do. She is "secret."

AP: Well, that's very good in this work.

O: She is people-knowing.

AP: Yes, extremely.

O: You must dispel all her foolish fears. Human fears. First, make
her understand the children's mission and your role. I take her
again by the hand and reveal myself. You may turn off your
machine—

AP: Yes, I will do that.

O: —or I shall have to.

AP: No, *I* will have to! We have ground rules. [*Machine is turned off for
a time, then continues.*]

O: Do not think of yourself as just a link. You are far, far more than
that. As the eagle flies, you too expand . . . but you know this,
dear Andrija.

AP: Yes.

O: So the circle expands, the energies grow. The shapes of things change.
Do you understand?

AP: Yes, I do. It is what we have been doing for a number of years.
We are ever expanding that circle of light. We need a few more,
don't we, to complete the circle?

O: Yes, but not that many. Instruct this one well. Guard her anonymity
for the time being.

AP: I understand how important that is to her.

o: That is where her greatest fear lies at the moment.

AP: That is where I can be helpful in shielding her. And Dick can too?

o: He will shield her in a most vital way, and he will be taught a unique method of so doing.

AP: What was Dick called? [*pause*] Is it important for Dick to go back to his home planet, too?

o: I do not think it necessary, much as she—Greta—would like for him to go. No, it is not necessary.

AP: What is the timetable to be for our work together?

o: Preparations are well under way. More about the coming of the gattae at another time, dear Doctor. I return the woman Greta to you. I do not know when we shall speak again. You will learn what you will from our Tauri. Never let her child's way fool you. Like the woman, Greta, she likes to play games. I go now. Begin your countdown.

So ended the one-hour session, and thus began a whole new chapter in our lives. Hearing the tape afterwards, I was startled by the melodious, male voice of Ogatta. I kept asking, as I had after our previous sessions, "That voice came through *my* vocal chords?" The incongruity of it all struck me, but I didn't know what to say about it, so I kept silent.

Andrija gently asked me to recount whatever I could recall of the past hour. "*Hour?*" I gasped. "Only an hour?" It had seemed an eternity to me while on Ogatta. Again, I realized that time is dimensional, and time and distance are relative terms when one travels in the Cosmos. What had been taped in an hour in the world of the third dimension, took me the rest of the day to explain to Andrija and Dick in detail, and even then most of it remained untold. I remember clearly thinking, "Is this really happening to me?" It was. It did. It is.

9

The Ogatta Group

T H E   D A Y S flew into nights as Andrija and Dick and I worked together, trying to sort out the information on tapes we had gathered from the various sessions. During one fascinating session, Hshames had given Andrija a fix in the globular-cluster identified as M-92 for his star catalogue calculations—another of the Good Doctor's many interests. In addition, Andrija asked Ogatta about an energy scheme he had developed for the Canadian Tesla Power Project. The answers he received were technical and involved items like "the c^2 envelope and helium." I, who managed to get through college and graduate with honors, while assiduously avoiding all but the required science courses, was totally lost in the playback on most of this. On the other hand, certain things fascinated me although I could not grasp them. I was given corrections on formulae, for instance, instructions to read things like Newton's Second Law of Thermodynamics. I strained to understand the concept of there being frequencies in plants to be used for healing the human body.

Another intriguing detail was that the members of the Ogatta group were, if one looked closely enough to notice, minutely feathered. Strangely enough, I saw and accepted it and thought little about it during and after the session. But both Dick and Andrija were intensely curious. It soon became obvious that those tiny feathers covering the Ogattan frames had a great deal of significance. Bits and pieces of dialogue indicated that this type of "skin" helped them become "part of the atmosphere," and they did not always "wear their feathers" when not on Ogatta.

Several years later we read of a presentation given at a Paris scientific conference (1975) in which magnetic sensitivity in birds was discussed. It was hypothesized that the sensitivity is in the feathers, which apparently act as transmission lines for energy at certain frequencies, while acting to insulate or block out other frequencies.

Our visitors from Ogatta told us that on the way station, Vesta, feathers were not needed. Much of this information came through Tauri who says it far more eloquently than I. I'll let her (as recorded by Dick) explain and tell us at the same time why Ogatta is both a person and a place.

T: I got here! I got here! I have to whisper to you [AP]. The place is *not* named after him, no. Silly fools used to name planets after what they thought were gods, and they were not gods, so the joke is on them. No, Ogatta was named for the planet, and not the other way 'round.

AP: Is there a planet named Tauri?

(This brought howls of high-pitched laughter, which pealed through the cage.)

T: I guess I have to go back to Vesta. They are all up there, and they want me to come back. My brothers want to talk to me. They just look at me and I *know*. I have to whisper to you [AP]. She doesn't really want to write and speak out down there. She wants her privacy. She is afraid the "world will move in on her children and husband." She thinks that, you know. It's not herself she worries about, it's family.

AP: Tell her we will protect her and she can use a different name. Our secret.

T: She doesn't see the significance of the first stages. When she starts to speak out, she will know those years of raising the family and building her marriage will give her all of the credibility she really needs. She doesn't see it yet. Her magnificent family connections will aid her in telling her cosmic connections! Same to be said for her business acumen.

AP: I understand. I will explain it to her. Dick will talk to her.

T: He [DICK] looks like Djemion but Lexitron is prettier!

AP: Who are they? Friends of yours? Are they boys or girls?

T: [*Peals of laughter again.*] We don't have *boys*, they are ingots. I'm an ingotta. Djemion and Lexitron are what *you'd* call my *brothers*. We're all on Vesta. Ugly old place. I want to go back to Ogatta. [*Longingly*] I want my feathers back.

AP: Well, I am sure you have a job to do there and when you have done it, you'll go back and get your feathers back when you arrive, right?

T: I like you. Look into her eyes. Open them up. Can you see me in there?

AP: I'm afraid not, Tauri. But I know you are very pretty.

T: I'm pretty? Oh, my goodness!

AP: Tauri, at the coming of the gattae, will you make yourself visible? Will you be seen in person or through our media? By other means?

T: I have to ask Ogatta what comes first.

AP: Is there to be any leader? Any godlike figure to appear with the coming of the gattae?

T: No! No! No! *All intelligence comes together.* It's a universal thing. There will be *no* deification this time. No!

AP: How will you communicate?

T: First by telepathy. She will be there, our channel. And you. *We* will not be first. We will guide others to your planet first. When the time is right, we will appear. More than twenty civilizations will be represented.

AP: When is that to be in our frame of reference?

T: The gattae will start to appear very soon. To small groups. No "press" as you call it will come of it. Then more and more will be seen, but they will not land on your ground for a while. In the coming decade the people on your planet will be prepared for the vibrations of the landings. In your time frame, much of the activity will be in the next one hundred moons.

AP: By a moon, do you mean a month?

T: Don't you know that? A moon is *almost* the same as what you call a month.

AP: I know I think you are too smart to be a little girl.

T: Ingotta! I'm an ingotta! And I am going back out there. Think of me as little.

AP: Goodbye, Tauri. I loved speaking with you. Thank you for visiting with us. Before you go, can you tell me one thing? What are you *doing* on Vesta?

T: Making loops. Lots of loops for the coming of the gattae.

AP: What are loops?

T: My goodness, *l-o-o-p-s*! Energy stones to power the gattae into your dimension! Do you want to see one? We make a lot of them, you know.

AP: I would like to see one very much! Are you smart enough to show me one?

T: Ogatta says I can take one. I can take—I can—

(Slowly, Greta's hand came up into the air, palm open, and suddenly on her fingertips lay a small, strangely colored stone the size of a lima bean.)

AP: May I hold it?

 T: Oh, you can keep it, if you want to!

AP: Yes, I do! Very much! Thank you. Tell me, what do I do with it?

 T: Why, you rub it and rub it and then there are two and that is all there is to it, once you have that kind of *first* one. I can make them, you know.

AP: Yes. Yes. It is technically impossible for any object to penetrate these specially constructed copper walls. Incredible the way you got it into this cage! Incredible!

 T: Your "womb of copper"? Ha-ha-ha!

AP: You are really something, Tauri. This loop literally appeared out of thin air, no pun intended. Would Ogatta mind if I had this stone analyzed in one of our laboratories far away?

 T: You can do anything you want to with it. The results may surprise you!

(Later analysis revealed that it was "not of any known origin.")

AP: What can we do for *you?*

 T: Help my channel to do what she is supposed to do for your planet before the coming of the gattae. Prepare her to trumpet the voice and scribe the pen. Make her know the—what do you call them—Space Kids? She chose to come back. Help her now and then she will have to soar it alone. But we will be there to help her once she can link into it with us.

AP: Yes, then she can go free and complete her job.

 T: As a child is born on your Planet Earth and takes nine months to come to be, so these next nine months at this start of your new year will be the birth for her. She will not lose her identity. One by one, we will make ourselves known to her. During the period of the coming of the gattae, everyone else who must know us will know also. Later. Later.

AP: What role will Richard her husband play, if any?

 T: He is her relay channel, so to speak. And he will be the scribe and keep the records for the future references. Dick will be her dear "Ezra"—yes! Like your "Ezra." I like games! I like analogies. I use analogies.

AP: You are a wonderful little person, Tauri!

T: I'm not so little. I'm big! Know how big? Want me to tell you how big in your inches or in maggots?

AP: Tell me in inches.

T: I'm almost forty-eight inches.

AP: Oh, now, that's terrific! Will you get Richard a stone too?

T: [*Ignoring that*] That's three maggots, you know.

AP: I am learning all kinds of things from you, Tauri. Can you teach me a few more things? You come from Ogatta but Hshames comes from Mennon. Are they close together? Who rules there? Can you tell me about it?

T: Ogatta is what you call the ruler. The boss. He is the Number One of all.

AP: All of what? What else does he boss or rule?

T: Why, Ogatta, Mennon, Tchauvi, Archa, and Oshan. Of course. Ogatta is the nicest of all, but they are all byoootiful. Vesta is an ugly place to have to be. It's boring! That's why I like to play games. Oh, and everything that is happening on Vesta, Ogatta bosses too. *Your* word, "boss."

AP: Thank you Tauri. You are going to keep things very lively around here, I can tell! Will you come back soon?

T: Try to make two loops from the one I gave you, okay? Bye.

AP: Goodbye. [*To* DICK] This is Vesta show biz! Amazing, isn't it? Look at how very different Greta's face is when she is not channeling.

D: I can't see a thing except the numbers on the clock.

AP: Next time sit over here, and if you lean way over, you can see her face. It changes physically depending on who is channeling through her. The face, the voice, it's all quite remarkably different. I will bring her out now. I wish I had asked if those four other places were planets like Ogatta.

Eventually we found out that Ogatta, Mennon, Archa, Oshan, and Tchauvi were indeed individual planets in a system rather foreign to our consciousness. They share two suns which orbit in unison. Our astronomers call this a binary or twin-star system.

Each of the five planets of the jorpah—Ogatta, Mennon, Archa, Oshan, Tchauvi—is more massive than our own Planet Earth, but much less dense than Earth. This is analogous to the Jupiter/Earth relationship. Jupiter has a mass 318 times that of Earth, but its average density is only 25 percent as great.

The five planets orbit on a plane or ecliptic between the two stars in the system. This differs from our own solar system where the planetary bodies orbit around the center of our system in which the Sun is so dominant that we say we orbit around the Sun.

Once in approximately 400 years, a total eclipse of one star by the others occurs in the jorpah. This eclipse lasts for an entire year, unlike the very brief periods that we experience eclipses in our system. During this period of eclipse the "light energy" available to the planets is much altered and brings about a suspension of a number of otherwise normal activities.

When I was fully back to my conscious state, Andrija probed to find out what "Greta" was doing while we talked to Tauri. "Where was she?" The transcript follows:

G: I had a most fabulous dream. I sort of zoomed out there! It was so real!

AP: Where did you end up? It *was* real, Greta, but think of it as a dream.

G: At the risk of sounding like a dingbat, I think it was another planet. I mean, I think it was Ogatta which *is* really another planet. My God!

AP: What did it look like?

G: Like huge dots. I mean, well, if you took a disc and covered it with halves of gorgeously iridescent marbles or halves of marbles—hemispheres—you might get the picture of what I saw. Like opals gleaming . . . colored dots. They hold something like water I think, and they are very precious.

AP: When you are there, do you transform into a different shape or form?

G: Yes, like that other tape said. Tiny little hairs of golden, velvety-looking feathers instead of skin. Like down, bronze-colored down that shines. And the marbles shine. Everything shines. Light surrounds you.

AP: Are the beings small?

G: Yes. About four feet or so, except for Ogatta who is a bit taller. And those *eyes*! He has got the most exquisite eyes I ever saw or dreamed of seeing. Speckled eyes with such . . . such . . . humanness and compassion and . . . and . . . well, *knowing* in them! And Andrija—Dick, darling—do you know that when I talk to them and they answer me, their mouths don't move at all. You know what they are saying but their mouths just do not move at all.

AP: Perhaps it's all telepathic? You know what they are saying. Did Ogatta speak to you? He said he would.

G: He kept raising my arm straight up into the air, and he told me that I shouldn't be concerned and that—I think what he was saying was that I have to go back to some kind of studies. With you, Andrija, but that I was under his protection and so were you. And that for a period of time, you would sort of protect me here.

AP: Uh-huh.

G: I don't really know in what way that will be.

AP: Just in a teacher-pupil relationship. That's all.

G: I'm to meet a lot of children, but they aren't all children or something.

AP: Yes.

G: I'm to see a room of people but I don't know who, and that you would clarify it so I shouldn't be afraid or concerned, because nobody else would know. Except Dick and my children.

AP: He had my word on that.

G: He said that all the persons in the circle would respect my privacy. I think that was the message. Oh, and that any time there was concern on my part, Dick and even my family would understand and be supportive, so I wasn't to fight it so much, I guess. I'll tell you something funny: when these people, these beings or entities, talk to you without moving their mouths . . . well, when they are displeased with your thinking, they do the strangest thing. I mean, they know what you are thinking, for god's sake. And if they are displeased with what you think, no less *say*, all their bones come up like this and hunch around their heads which sort of sink down onto their chests like this, and they moan! *That*, you can *hear*! It's not telepathic, you can hear them.

AP: That's marvelous!

G: And it's like "MMMMMmmmmmmmmmMMMMMMmmmmmm," and their feathers come up! It kind of tickled me, which annoyed the deuce out of them, but that's all right. They knew me and welcomed me and loved me. Oh, lord, what a weird experience. I don't know that I would have wanted to come back at all, but Dick and the children are here, so I wouldn't stay out there.

AP: Yes. Rest now. We are finished working for a while. You are doing just magnificently, and Dick and I are thrilled with the progress you are making.

I was thrilled too. And perhaps because of my elation, I was not the least bit tired. But I *was* hungry, and I concluded the morning by giving into my very human urge to have lunch. *And* dessert.

10

Dear Ezra

THE OGATTA GROUP had given Dick the name Ezra. It was one of our names, they said, and indeed it is. The Old Testament gives prominent mention to Ezra, one of the great reformers of Judaic law. He was known as Ezra the Scribe and it was said of him, "Just as he was the scribe of the words of the law, so he was the scribe of the words of the sages."

From my first day of channeling, Dick—my Ezra—was told that he must chronicle and remember what he saw and heard. "She consciously blocks" was a frequent complaint from my extraterrestrial friends about me, so Dick was commissioned to become the eyes and ears. He was told early on that in a few years I would write a book, and his scribings would be the basis from which it would spring. He was also told that "Greta doesn't doubt our existence, she doubts her own worthiness." Andrija understood this syndrome, the *"Why me?"* stage, since he had been through the same soul-searching process with others as well as with himself. There is no answer, by the way, to *"Why* me?" and "Why *me?"* And yet I ask it when the positives occur through healings, predictions, materializations. I keep asking it when the negatives become oppressive through peer pressure and ridicule, physical upheavals and changes in my body, exhaustion. *"Why me?"*

From the outset, ground rules had to be established and they came about in a rather amusing way. While Tauri and others from the Ogatta group wanted Dick to write down and remember what was transpiring, they also scolded him good-naturedly for relying too heavily on tapes.

"You don't listen," he was told. "You have a beautiful mind, but if you come to depend on machines and on the pen, then you forget to think and to relate and that is not good." Or, "You listen but you do not hear, because you are fussing."

They also devised a few tricks to emphasize their point. In the beginning, poor Dick would tape the conversations, play them for me, go to transcribe the tape and, wham! the tape would be gone. Kaput. Vanished. "Dematerialized." After just such an event one evening, Dick had the following dialogue with Tauri:

D: May I use my tape machine tonight?

T: No. Next time I may blow up the machine instead of just taking the tape.

D: Tauri, you're too much! Isn't it beneficial for Greta to hear the tapes? She has no memory of our conversations because she is "out there" when you use her vehicle. She wants to hear *you*. Won't you agree that it's easier for her when I can play the tape for her?

T: Logic is on your side.

D: Please don't play games with them any more. Tell me to erase them and I will, if you prefer it, after Greta hears them and I transcribe them. Whatever you say, but please don't dematerialize them, Tauri.

T: Just so that you train yourself to remember and be able to bring the necessary information to her. Here's your silly old tape back.

At this point, the tape fell from nowhere and landed on the bald spot on top of Dick's head. Later, when he played the tape it was all there, except for one small section in the middle which the ETI had chosen to delete.

T: "Blows your mind?" Is that your lingo? Blows your mind?

D: [Laughing] Tauri, you are just too much!

T: Well, all right, I won't take your tapes, but I *will* blow up the machine unless you listen and hear and *then* use the tapes to sharpen the details.

D: It's a deal, Tauri. Greta will be so glad; she adores listening to you on tape every bit as much as I do. I wish I could see you as she can.

T: Look deep into the eyes of the channel and one day you will see *me* in there. Maybe not now, but one day.

D: [Looking into channel's eyes] I cannot see you but I know you are pretty. I know how much I like you.

T: Thank you. It's nice to be liked.

D: Are you concerned about being liked on Ogatta?

T: On Ogatta I am loved.
D: We love you, Tauri.

From the beginning, Dick and Tauri had easy dialogues which went from light and bandying to serious and thought-provoking. They teased one another with little thought of the dimensions that separated them. When I listened to the tapes, I was constantly struck by the tender quality of the exchanges, no matter what the subject. To this day, Tauri still threatens to "blow up the machine" when she instructs Dick to let me hear it and then erase it. She has never gone that far, but what she does do frequently is jam the mechanism, especially if someone walks into the room while a tape is on that she doesn't want them to hear. It's really quite funny. The machine simply will not play. The person leaves, and the tape rolls on.

I recently found out that when there is a line or two that Tauri doesn't want me to hear, she "assists me" into a fit of sneezing that precludes my catching the lines. My children get absolutely convulsed with laughter when this happens, but I become very cranky. Such is the lighter side of the ETI. "Keep it light" is a favorite theme of theirs, and they practice what they preach. I teach the same theme to my students in the yoga, psi research, and energy classes I conduct.

The ETI assigned Dick a role that he assumed graciously and faithfully from the beginning. This transcript from February 21, 1977, describes that role succinctly:

T: Act as a reporter, not as a feature writer, Dick. Stand back, observe, and report what you have heard to the channel when she is back with you. Do not embroider . . . embellish . . . report it simply. Being a reporter is good for the soul. Be accurate. Remember what you hear. Being a "reporter" is good for the soul!
D: If that is how I can be the most helpful, I shall be a reporter.
T: Good. You may not believe me now, but your business will become secondary to this work. What you will do is vital. Her business will suffer a bit; that is the way it has to be. She can cut back in the number of her clients and still have a good company. The Ogatta group will be taking her out of her body more and more often now that she has agreed to cooperate. As an astronaut has a "life-support system" when he goes out in space, you, dear Dick, will act as umbilicus to Greta as she goes forth in the work. She calls you her "Power Pack." Have we not talked about that before? A prime force for

energy is love. You will protect her vehicle and she can soar with confidence. This is not the time to go into it, but let me mention that hate is also a prime mover of energy, and neither love nor hate as such should ever be minimized.

D: Are you saying that I provide a love energy as a protection screen around Greta's body when she is not "in it"?

T: Exactly. And you shall learn to do it well, I am sure. One must not leave the channel open—unguarded—vulnerable. There are "kookies" out there who look for such an opportunity. Never mind that for now. You will do very well. Love is an energy. Laughter is an energy. You have an abundance of both to give to your "bride," as you call her.

D: She *is* my bride! She will be my bride of twenty-five years this year. Twenty-five beautiful years.

T: Yes. Yes. Oh, my goodness, we *do* pick our people well.

As the days flowed into weeks and months, Dick and Tauri developed a special rapport. Dick may have been dubbed a reporter and scribe in the eyes of the Ogatta group, but he in turn subjected each entity to the probings of his highly inquisitive mind. Dick never lost an opportunity to prod for answers to his own questions in order to attain a better understanding of what was happening to me.

D: How marvelous that you came in, Tauri. I've been concentrating on you. You haven't talked to me for a long time. Could you hear me calling?

T: I would have to wait a long, long time if I had to wait for the sound of your *voice*. I receive your thought vibrations, though, in the blink of an eye.

D: Can you give me an idea as to how fast those thought vibrations travel? In our measurements? Faster than the speed of light? How fast?

T: I should think you would be satisfied to know that we out here can hear you at all! I should think you would be excited over the fact that out here somebody is even looking at you, you drop of water in the sea, you! Everything in good time. Formulae. You are thinking about that $E = mc^2$ aren't you, you insignificant thing?

D: It's a good thing you are laughing or I'd be hurting!

T: Not you, not you. I tease a lot. I laugh a lot. And I hear you and your questions, but I am not going into that now. Later, yes. Now, no. Certain of your mysteries I cannot unlock for you, but then again the definition of science is only two words: *cosmic revelations.* The information is all out there, and you know it is, and all one has to learn is to latch on to it. Let me put it to you this way: there was fission and fusion long before there was your Mr. Einstein.

D: The definition of science is cosmic revelation. Marvelous!

T: It's also the definition of "miracles." Miracles are just cosmic revelations, and miracles "occur" every day. [*Pause*] Of course, the biggest miracle will be to get her going—my channel. Andrija must lead her and you must structure her as you both promised to do. She is reluctant to get going. Push, but not too hard. There are to be more and more times in the coming moons for you to guard her well. When the spirit soars, no matter how far or near, the body becomes an empty vessel, and anything can fill it. Always be on guard lest they sap and suck her energy.

D: Who are "they"? How can they do that? Where do they come from?

T: Stop! Stop! I am taking all of this off the tapes. She doesn't have to concern herself with "kookies" and neither do you. Just be aware and wary. I tease you about your questions, but I am glad that you are open to answers and open-minded; and all the questions that *can* be answered *will* be in good time, I promise you. Yours is a difficult role in that you have no memory of what was before, nor will you have. You are not, yourself, an active "psychic" or channel, but rather a relay for Greta. This would frustrate the most ordinary of men. Egos and all that. But not you, dear Dick, not you. You accept your role and play it out as you, too, agreed to do at one point in time. Yes, you are one of my favorite human beings.

D: Thank you. No, I don't mind not *doing* what Greta does, although I'd love to see some of the sights she does. I would love to see you, little Tauri.

T: Look deeply into my channel's eyes, and one day you will, you will.

D: I am content with things as they are. I really am. When any of you come through, it is a wonderful experience each and every time. I'm awed to be a part of that and I really *am* content. If I went "out there" I don't know that I'd be able to maintain the steady balance that Greta does. I am aware of how difficult it is for her to lead two lives. She really does sort of lead two lives, you know?

T: The Ogatta group picks its people well. Yes.

After our initial three days at Lab Nine in December, Dick and I spent a quiet New Year's Eve explaining what had transpired to our four children. All had foregone their usual Christmas vacation skiing trips in order to hear about my adventures in Ossining.

It was a typical family reunion, with the Big Four, each with his or her own very distinctive personality, clowning, rehashing old times, and enjoying each other's company. Born within five years of each other, they had grown up almost as quadruplets. Perhaps that's why they have always supported each other emotionally, physically, and even financially when necessary. And why they've also been known to form a wall of solidarity on an issue, when they deemed it necessary.

Our four children have made parenthood easier than Dick and I had a right to expect, and many a friend, neighbor, relative, and acquaintance has commented, with pleasure, a touch of jealousy, and occasionally shock, on how they act more like best friends than siblings.

January 3, 1977, found us all gathered around the brunch table exchanging views on the past few days' events. The Big Four had all pored over the transcripts of the initial sessions, and Dick and I did our best to expand the notes, so we could give them whatever further thoughts and insights we had. From the start, I was stubbornly reluctant to read any of the material or listen to any of the tapes more than once. My reason was simple: I wanted any and all memory of the ETI channeling to be first-hand and uncomplicated by repetition. While my family thought me foolish, I remained adamant and did not read what was to become more than one thousand pages of scribing until the time came—over two years later—to start writing this book.

Later on that January day, my three oldest children returned to their respective colleges. After they left, I lay down on the couch and "nodded off," as Dick came to call my out-of-the-cage channeling. Suddenly, Tauri's voice came through and Ann, my youngest, became the first of our children to meet this delightful being.

Tauri told her about a young girl (ingotta) named Maya, who was on Vesta at the time, and with whom Ann had a close connection. Maya apparently knew all about Ann and watched her frequently. Tauri assured us that Maya would watch Ann on her travels abroad.

Ann thought this amusing, but her facial expression also indicated some degree of skepticism. She had no plans to travel abroad and no idea what Tauri was talking about. Three months later we all found out.

Ann, who was then a senior in high school, had more than enough credits to graduate early. Soon after her visit from Tauri, she decided that she would like to spend six months abroad before entering Dartmouth in the fall. The following are excerpts from a letter Ann sent us from Israel that April.

Danny [a friend she met on the trip] and I were returning to Kiryat Ata from Mount Carmel at 12:45. We were in an Israeli invention known as the *sherut*, which is like a taxicab which follows the bus routes, picks up passengers at the stops, and charges per seat. It costs less than private cabs, is a great deal roomier (seating only seven), and goes faster.

Our *sherut* was full and was swinging down the winding road two kilometers from the central section of Haifa when a car approached us, coming from around a curve. From that moment, it seemed as though the accident took place in slow motion for me. My instinct was to throw my arm in front of Danny's body to brace him from lunging forward. Running through my mind was the thought that we were in the most suicidal seats, since Dan was directly behind the driver and I was next to him in the middle seat. A bar runs across the back of the *sherut* behind the driver's seat for middle-seat passengers to hold onto. My right hand went to the bar and my left went up to protect Danny. We were going about 30 mph; I let out a scream and turned my head to Danny just before the car was about to hit us.

The next thing I knew, I was looking *down* at the accident. Mom, Dad, I know that sounds crazy, but it's true. It was as though I had been lifted somehow out of my body and allowed to *watch* the collision. Immediately after the *sherut* and car crashed, the next thing I remembered was being on the other side of the street, walking with Danny in the opposite direction of the wreck. I had no recollection of how we got there, nor did I feel injured, despite the obvious minor lacerations I could see. Danny turned to me and in his broken English (he's a Russian immigrant, you know) asked me if I had somehow "seen the accident from above or the sky." His question shocked me speechless! The same thing had happened to him!

I knew I was being protected in Israel after what Tauri had said when

I first met her, but the shock of the situation was that Danny had experienced the same thing and had questioned me without it fazing him in the least!

Don't worry about me. I was more than fortunate—we both were—to walk away with just minor lacerations, considering the aftermath of the accident. The head-on collision shattered the front windshield and caused the instant death of the driver, the front-seat passenger, and the left back-seat passenger. The other three were injured and hospitalized.

We went to the hospital for a routine check and to have our lacerations treated and after answering police questions, we were released, being told it was a "miracle we survived the crash the way we did." I was shook up but I don't know what did it more . . . the fact that three were killed? . . . the fact that Danny and I both experienced what we did? . . . the fact that I had been told back in January that Tauri (or was it Maya?) would watch me during my traveling? . . . all I know is that I *was* protected somehow, and I am here to tell you that all is fine.

What Ann did *not* know was that at the exact time of the accident, Tauri took over the channel and informed us that Ann was "safe and sound thanks to Maya's intervention at the time of a car accident." We were not to worry, Tauri told us, but since Ann "would feel the urge to call home," we should be alerted to her state of high anxiety. She called (collect, naturally!) and we began to probe immediately. She asked with wonderment how we *possibly* could have known about the wreck. Long-distance prices being prohibitive, we told her briefly, then rung off a few minutes later, satisfied that our youngest child was well.

That quick conversation with Tauri on January 3 was the first channeling by ETI that we had without "scientific conditions" and without warning. From that time on, the channeling was to continue in the strangest of places and at some of the oddest moments. The ETI—all fourteen of them—were rapidly to become regular members of our family, popping in and out to interject thoughts into various conversations. It was as though they were establishing their credibility with us. They were, in fact, doing more than that. Over the years there were times when I would still question their abilities and technology. As E. F. Schumacher says, "If in doubt show it prominently. All matters that are beyond doubt are in a sense dead; they constitute no challenge to the living." It was on the occasions when I would question the very existence of the ETI when indeed they would establish their "credibility."

"So you think we are a fiction of your mind, do you? Well, can *you* do *this*?" Awis might ask—and almost every piece of furniture in my living room would be instantly rearranged (including a 300-pound marble statue). "No! Oh, how did you do that?" And with a short, tinkling laugh, the furniture would be set back into place in front of our startled eyes. "Can *you* do this all by yourself and not as a channel?" little Omee would ask—and a long-lost item would appear on one of our shoulders or hands. "Or this, perhaps?" smilingly from Cjork—as we'd watch a burned-out candle spring into flame and burn steadily for a full day in a glass without wax or wick visible. "Listen *once* to your tape, for thereafter it will be no more," Renjavi could caution—and after hearing the playback, and rewinding, the tape would be blank. And of course, all that metal which "bends" all around me, I know is linked to one of the Ogatta group. Yes, they established their credibility with each and every one of the six pragmatists in our family. Indelibly. Deliciously.

11

Blinking Starward

AFTER Tauri's chat with Ann and Dick, I suggested that we get in touch with Dr. Puharich and tell him what had happened. Andrija was quite surprised to hear of this turn of events. He and Dick had a long discussion about what it meant and how such encounters should be handled in the future. Afterward, I refused to let Dick tell me what Andrija had said. I am naturally a curious person, but I deliberately "turned off" hearing any secondhand news about the ETI. The only thing I *did* ask about was the safety methodology by which Dick was trained to bring me back after channeling, should there be a delay of any kind once an entity left the channel.

The answer regarding Dick's maneuvers came not from Andrija, but from our guide and mentor, Abdul, who had spoken with Andrija at our first meeting. According to the Good Doctor, Abdul was a highly developed soul who had been a doctor in Basra, a port in southeastern Iraq, about sixty miles from the head of the Persian Gulf. That Abdul had at one time been Eileen Garrett's guide pleased me immeasurably.

Two or three weeks after Ann's amazing experience in Israel, Dick and his partner had to go to California on a business trip. They thought perhaps their wives would enjoy coming along and we wholeheartedly agreed. I put some of my business affairs in order before leaving. Others were taken along. The joy of my executive search firm is that I can conduct a goodly portion of my work wherever there is a telephone.

Some very interesting things happened on that trip, beginning at our first stop, Carmel. We knew that Andrija was working on a new book about the man who turned down a Nobel Prize—researcher, inventor, and consultant on energy matters, Nikola Tesla.

Dick was anxious to learn more about Tesla and his plan for obtaining unlimited energy from the atmosphere. We were unaware that a biography of the scientist was already in print, but wandering down a side street one afternoon, we stumbled on a bookstore. We went in to browse, and there, on an upper shelf, was a single copy of *Prodigal Genius, The Life of Nikola Tesla.* The shopkeeper told us that it was the only one he had. Moreover, he himself proved to be immensely knowledgeable about Tesla's work. Dick was delighted and engaged the man in a lively and lengthy conversation. Coincidence.

Some days later we were in San Francisco, and we unsuccessfully tried to locate one of Dick's cousins in the Greater San Francisco telephone book. (We found out later that he lived in Marin County.) That very night, while parking the car in a garage off an alley leading to Ghirardelli Square, Dick heard someone call his name. He looked, and there was his cousin, Bob, in a million-to-one chance meeting, in the alley way. Coincidence.

Another evening I was showering when I heard the phone ring. Dick, who was shaving over the sink, mumbled, "Who could that be?" Since we had told no one but our children the name of the hotel where we would be staying, he couldn't imagine.

"Pick it up," I called, "and say hello to Goldie for me, too." I heard Dick say, "Hello." Then, with amazement in his voice, he asked, "How are you, Goldie?" It was, as I had foreseen, my sister-in-law. She had tracked us down by calling one of our children. Coincidence.

As I told you earlier, I like games of chance. One of the high spots of our trip was to be a visit to one of the casinos in Lake Tahoe. On the day we were to go, Dick took four silver dollars and put them in his top drawer before lunch. When he returned to our room less than an hour later, he found only three. I had not seen or touched them. That night at the casino Dick won over one hundred dollars. When he went to cash in his chips, he noticed that he had only a single one dollar bill. He made a careful mental note of this, since we would be leaving the next morning and he knew he would need the dollar to tip the bellboy. When we got back to our room, Dick checked his wallet before dropping it into the dresser drawer, and was flabbergasted to see that the lone dollar bill was gone. I assured him there was nothing to get excited about. There had to be some rational explanation for the dollar's disappearance. With that, I stretched out on the bed, "nodded off," and there was Tauri.

T: I got you your stupid old cousin and that made you happy, did it? Well, since I can't play games with those bones [dice] I can play others. Look in Greta's wallet in front of the pieces of paper. So much for "coincidence." Ask her before you look what she has in *her* wallet in singles and silver dollars, okay? Some cosmic proof for the two of you of what can be done!

When I opened my eyes and was "with it" after the ritual Dick always went through, he asked me if I had any money in my wallet. Naturally, I did not know that I had been used as a channel. When entities come in and out for quick comments, I am totally unaware of what is happening. In fact, I generally pick up my thought or sentence exactly where I left off when the being took over my vehicle. This might be anywhere from a minute to an hour later and invariably provokes peals of hysteria from my children. I generally respond with a grumpy look, although privately I must admit that the kids have a right to laugh. I would if I were in their place.

Dick asked if I had any singles or silver dollars and I replied, "Two of each." I knew I was right because I had seen them when I put the money I won at the casino—which was all in tens—behind them. Dick asked me to open my wallet and show him. When I did, I found three singles and three silver dollars. Somehow Dick's missing dollar bill and silver dollar had found their way into *my* wallet.

Tauri also told Dick a few other things during that visit:

T: So, you are going to read some things about Tesla? He doesn't concern you as he does the Good Doctor.
D: Did you lead me to the book, Tauri?
T: "Coincidences, coincidences!" You don't *have* to know all about him though. Tell the Good Doctor to *look into the uranium*. Not Tesla now.
D: I'm sorry, I didn't catch that. Look into uranium did you say?
T: Yes. Look into the uranium thing. Germ warfare plays its part. The other man will understand. Yes.

After Dick explained Tauri's role in the wallet episode and told me about her message on uranium, I insisted that we call Andrija immediately. Our notes from that trip indicate that it was 1:15 P.M., which would have made it 4:15 P.M. in New York. Andrija got very agitated when Dick told him what Tauri had said about the uranium. Only he and one other person knew about a potentially dangerous supply of uranium used in a secret project that had taken place some five months before. They had been told that when the time came for them to "do something about it," they would "get a message."

While Andrija was explaining this to us, a unique thing happened in our hotel room. There were three lights on: one on the telephone table, one overhead, and one in the far corner of the room, near a table and two easy chairs. *All the lights* blinked on and off simultaneously. All the switches to the lights were in different places in the room, and Dick and I were both sitting on the bed and hadn't touched any of them. Andrija took this as a confirmation of his interpretation that the time to do something was *now*. He said no more about it, thanked us hurriedly, and hung up. We never asked him about his secret project again, nor did he ever volunteer any further information.

The next night we were in Los Angeles. Tauri visited and reiterated that she loved to play games:

T: Never mind the flip form that I take from time to time. At the moment I have something to tell you, and please do not concern yourself with interpreting my message, which is for the Good Doctor. *She* is a channel and *you*, dear Dick, take the messages as they are given. Ingest them; do not ever be fearful, and scribe them down.

D: I will be careful to do as you say. What is the message for Dr. Puharich?

T: E.R.D.A. Erda. He can think Tesla. Tell him about the big mirrors from E.R.D.A. They could be duplicated in this country. Mirrors from E.R.D.A. for energy from the Sun. Do you know that they have great big mirrors in the forest? Hshames knows all about that. Now, since you will carry the message for me, I will do something for you. Yes, FIRNA!

The room was suffused with an orangy, almost lilac-y aroma, a delightful scent that we soon came to associate with any of the Ogatta group at their sweetest. We called Andrija with this latest information but we had no further messages from Tauri until we returned from our trip, and I again visited Lab Nine. The date was January 28, 1977.

AP: What was the urgency in your messages when Dick and Greta were out West?

T: I'll let you talk to Hshames about that. Let him [DICK] just listen because he pounds everything into the ground with all his questions!

H: I shall tell you about the E.R.D.A. message now. The heat of the Sun is available to 2,000 degrees of your Fahrenheit, and can liquidize the vapor to generate electricity. The Sun's energy is yet another matter. Now to E.R.D.A. [Energy Research and Development Association] and the solar electric plant that is being planned. They consider just the *heat* of the Sun and you only receive less than half of the Sun's rays due to clouds. Half of the Sun's rays are not known. The *light* from the Sun when on certain crystals can create electricity directly. Not through vapor to generate your turbines. You know all this from the spacecraft developed on your planet. The problem in your space program with this is strictly financial. The cost per watt costs many of your dollars, not fractions of cents! Just consider what a shingle on your house would be—a crystal shingle to convert light to electricity directly. But back to the mirrors . . . 400–500 mirrors in a forest . . . one receiver on a tower . . . realize that this could produce the equivalent of 3,000 of your suns in heat power.

AP: Can you give us a cheap solar collector material? What may we consider?

H: Consider what was done in miniaturizing transistors. It went from dollars to pennies per unit.

AP: We do not know the material to use to withstand the rays of the Sun year after year.

H: Forget the rays of the Sun! Think in terms of the *light of the Sun!* And know that electric companies must become more concerned with the *storage* than they are. The storage is the key to the business aspects of it.

AP: We need efficient collectors and energy storage.

H: In the Sun belt but not necessarily in the center of the Earth.

AP: The equator!

H: This is not meant for *this* channel, really. Think in terms of three months ahead when your old administration is leaving and you can come into play with all of this. I leave you now.

AP: I thank you most sincerely, Hshames. I have a great deal to think about.

We all had a great deal to think about. To be a willing channel meant allowing entities from the Ogatta group to come and go with my blessings. Free will always did (and still does) play a tremendous part in the scheme of things. One is never robbed of free will. I knew I could choose to be unavailable as a channel and our ETI friends would respect that decision. But, I trusted my ETI and let them use my vehicle freely, always knowing that Dick would guard my body well when I was "out there."

At times, no one would frequent my body while I was "out there," being instructed in various matters. Then my vehicle would be "empty." I must confess that free will and my exercise of it were questionable to me at first. Only over a period of time did I come to realize and appreciate my control over my availability as a channel. Here is an example of how it works.

T: There are times my channel does not feel she has control of the situation. That bothers her. I watch this with more than a casual interest. If ever she has a doubt in her mind about her free will, let her face the fact that *she has the doubt,* and no one—no being—interferes in any way. She has her free will, total free will, in what she chooses to do with her time, and with her mind, with her body. She has free will in what she chooses to do with her commitments. While we in the Ogatta group select our people well, we nonetheless stay back and watch and wait and listen and evaluate. We wish we could change the free will many times, but we don't. No. Other times we say "Bravo!" Human she is, and in human terms she must make her decisions regarding free will in regard to accessibility. It is her choice.

There were times when our questions to ETI became personal. We would ask for specific answers to mundane problems, and inevitably would receive gentle but firm chastisement. Here is an excerpt from a January 1978 transcript which had come after many weeks of *no* channeling.

T: I do not like to see sadness in the eyes of my channel or in your eyes, dear Dick. I hear you "screaming for me" out there! Know that I cannot take over the channel just to talk about things that do not concern the work we do, and that you have committed to do. It would be wrong for me to do so. There is a law and an order in the Universe, and you must recognize that as a fact. I cannot come to answer your direct questions which have no direct bearing on our mission. It would be improper to expect extraterrestrial interference or intervention because, you see, the type of answers you seek deprive you of your free will in decision-making. We are all comfortable with each other at this point. When questions take on—assume—a totally "human level," they are wrong questions. Do you understand me, Dick?

D: Ah, Tauri, you shame us all for our unspoken, personal questions.

T: Do not be shamed. Be aware of the importance of free will. *And know that our silence and delays are not denials.* No. And I did not forget you!

Even now, years later, prolonged periods of silence continue to unsettle us. We should know better.

T: Know that one of the saddest things when dealing with humans is the need for words. In the dimensions of no language—in the spheres of thought and reception where concepts are delivered without the use of words—everything is understood more readily. Can you understand how much more can be accomplished—and on a much larger scale? As for you and my channel, you are humans and therefore "grounded" as it were. Each human must learn to stand on his or her own feet and must walk alone. Strong. Always know that we will not intervene on your human questions, for no course of action is *ever* given to you. *We will give direction* but *never directives.* You exist on a dimension full of meaningless words. But when words *have* meaning which you have absorbed, you can then forget the words and hold on to the concept.

And, finally, one brief encounter which brought with it this message which lingered long in our memories for its lesson on free will:

T: Most human beings need to creep before they walk, walk before they run. Don't rush things so. You ask for answers to too many questions which are not relevant to the work at hand. And for the queries which *do* apply, many are premature in that you have not prepared yourselves sufficiently to receive answers. And answers from us you will not receive in any case. My dear children, the hardest thing for you all to comprehend is why the vital information stops when you need it most, or think you do. Don't you all realize that should we give you a direct course of action to follow, all of your free will would disappear? More important, your learning to "think and relate" would not have its full "play." It's vital that you think things out for yourselves. I'd be wrong to upset that necessary procedure and balance. You know, it's rather peculiar, we can divulge *universal truths* but not workaday solutions. If only you knew how fortunate that is for you! Bye.

As 1977 got under way, Dick and I had a great deal to think about. We had been assured of training by both humans and ETI in work aimed at guiding humankind through the difficult years ahead. We had little to gain personally and much to lose in making a commitment for the coming year. Time. Energy. Money. The latter two we could spare, but we already had so little time to do the things that life demanded of us.

The children and Dick felt that as far as I was concerned, it was a simple matter of priorities. They urged me to commit the year then and there to this work. Then, as now, I marvel at those individuals who do not have a "Dear Ezra" or sympathetic children to encourage them. Reassured by my eager and supportive family gathered around me, commit for a year I did. It turned out to be a major decision and one that I have never regretted. Well, almost never.

12

Global Rumblings

I COMMITTED MYSELF to working with the Good Doctor, to learning all that I could about sensory perception that at the current "state of the art" was being called paranormal; and to forging the strongest ties possible with my newfound friends in the Cosmos. Simultaneously, Dick and I set about seeking any information that would shed some light on Andrija's bleak prognosis for the coming decades.

The information we found supported the Scenario. A sampling of the evidence we uncovered in books, magazines, newspapers, television programs is herein provided. All sustain the picture of change painted for our planet between now and the year 2000.

"The face of this planet is changing," Alfred Webre and Phillip Liss state in their book, *The Age of Cataclysm*:

There are signs that the climate of the earth and the forces within the earth may destructively impinge on human society with a force unprecedented in recent human history. The earth appears to be entering a period of vast changes in climatic and geologic systems. These are changes that are largely unforeseen by human policy-makers, and for which our present social systems are generally unprepared. If in reality the earth is headed for an age of cataclysm, the rapid development of the earth sciences seems critical to humanity's plans for survival.

Geologists, our students of the good ship Planet Earth, tell us that *plate tectonics* will change the face of our planet. The Earth's crust consists of twenty plates which resemble large rafts floating on molten rocks of the Earth's interior. Tectonics refers to the deformation of the Earth's crust. If you look at Africa and South America, you can see that the shapes of the two continents appear to fit as two pieces of a jigsaw puzzle. If you take the three pieces that constitute North America, Greenland, and Eurasia, you will find that they also make a good fit in the puzzle. The estimates of the break-up of Africa and South America are between 100 and 200 million years ago, while the separation that made North America, Greenland, and Eurasia occurred over 100 million years ago.

Earthquakes and volcanoes are associated with the "lines of weakness"—fault lines—in the Earth's crust where the plates meet. Although earthquake activity has played a continuing part throughout human history, there has been a definite acceleration in the last two decades. Major cities around the world have been, and are, situated along well-defined fault lines, with major segments of the world's population settled atop these seismic arsenals. Similar growth has occurred along the San Andreas fault in California where the major cities of Los Angeles and San Francisco now boast populations in the many millions.

For example, since the last major earthquake in Japan in 1923, which took 143,000 lives, the Toyko–Yokohama area has grown into one of the largest, if not the largest, metropolitan area in the world. Furthermore, most of the land mass of Japan is crisscrossed by major active fault systems.

Both North, South, and Central America, from Alaska to the southern tip of Argentina, lie along juncture points of tectonic plates. Because of this, Guatemala and Nicaragua have experienced major quakes over the past few years. (You may recall the one in Managua, Nicaragua, in 1972; baseball hero Roberto Clemente was killed when his plane crashed while flying food and medical supplies to the devastated city.)

What I find most interesting about earthquakes is that damage to property and loss of life is rarely due to the tremor of the Earth itself, but to the consequences of the tremor—the large-scale fires, floods, structural collapses, and, of course, the inevitable panic.

Since we have many friends living in California, I have made a study of that state. Reports indicate dangerous times ahead. The western side of the San Andreas fault is part of the Pacific plate, while the rest of the state and country are on the American plate. The American plate is drifting in a direction just north of due west, while the Pacific plate is drifting in a northwest direction. Not only does this make southern California more seismically active than any other part of the United States, it makes it more seismically active than any other area on Earth!

Peter Franken of the University of Michigan, formerly Acting Director of the Pentagon's Advanced Research Projects Agency, is quoted as saying that "any seismologist will in fact be surprised if a major earthquake does not occur in the next ten years in California. And the impact would be large. Fatalities would number several tens of thousands." The injured and the later fatalities would number hundreds of thousands.

Physicists John Gribbin and Stephen Plageman of Cambridge University, co-authors of *The Jupiter Effect*, emphasize in their book that a major earthquake can be triggered in California by the alignment of the Sun and the planets in the mid-1980s. They suggest the Los Angeles region as the most likely area for this earthquake, and further conjecture that it could be the most massive ever experienced by a major population center in this century.

This earthquake activity along the San Andreas fault is common knowledge. Whenever California is discussed, in fact, earthquake jokes pop up in the conversation. I've even heard Californians tell stories on themselves; one couple built a house directly over the fault line so everyone in the family could have his own "separating space."

I have lectured in four cities in California, soliciting excellent questions from members of my "corporate" audiences, but not one man wished to discuss seismic-activity possibilities. "I'll take my chances" seemed to be the ostrich attitude of these entrepreneurs. They accepted the concept of ETI more easily than the concept of destruction to their enterprises or homes.

Oddly enough, people never seem to see the impending danger in terms of their own safety—which points up some of the problems involved when you know where disaster will strike. In one of Dick's conversations with Tauri, she noted that a major city appeared to be marked for destruction by one of the natural forces that will be unleashed on Planet Earth. Dick begged her to tell him the name of the city. If we knew, we could go there and warn the inhabitants of the impending disaster. Tauri's response:

Dick, do you think that those you would speak to would leave their homes and businesses and the rest of their materials on just the words of you and my channel? No, I don't either. They would want to know the exact time and date and month, and then; even with that information, how many of them do you think would leave? Not very many, I'm afraid. No, it wouldn't do much good 'for my channel to know the location of what she saw . . . and we certainly would never roll the screen to give exact dates and times. Best forget about trying to warn those directly in the line of one of the catastrophes before it happens.

Tauri was right, of course. How could anyone ever convince people in an area marked for disaster that they should move? People become attached to their homes and possessions and are not easily persuaded to give them up. Another problem: where would you move these potential earthquake victims?

On July 28, 1976, the city of Tangshan was demolished by the deadliest earthquake experienced by the Chinese in four centuries. An article in *The New York Times* on June 2,1977, recounted the details which the Chinese kept secret for the better part of a year. The earthquake reportedly took the lives of more than 750,000 people and leveled the major industrial and coal-producing area 100 miles from Peking.

Tauri told us, however, that the death toll had actually been even more staggering. In response to Dick's query about the number of victims, she replied:

TAURI: High numbers. There are six zeros in there.
DICK: Six zeros! That's over a million people!
TAURI: It did what it was to do. And it was "one of many such phenomena that must occur on Planet Earth."

The Tangshan earthquake occurred without any warning, so the population could not be evacuated—which is odd, because the Chinese invest a tremendous amount of money and manpower in earthquake studies and predictions. They have hundreds of workers mobilized on a full-time basis in each province, which adds up to hundreds of thousands across the country. We saw this for ourselves when we were in China in November 1978, and it was eerily impressive.

In addition, the Chinese have made extensive studies of animal behavior in line with the age-old contention that animals have early warning systems that let them know when earthquakes are imminent.

In 1975 Chinese earthquake experts—using a forecasting system that combined animal behavior reports with seismic and atmospheric indicators—were able to move thousands of people out of Haicheng twenty-four hours before it was struck by a major quake. Despite their expertise in these matters, the Chinese were unable to foresee the awful cataclysm at Tangshan.

The use of animal behavior in earthquake predicting has stepped up considerably in the past twenty years. In addition to the Chinese studies, the Japanese have been doing their work using special species of fish. These fish perceive changes in the Earth's electromagnetic field prior to earthquakes. Russian scientists have picked up on these animal indicators and have amassed a great deal of carefully documented information. Their studies include the habits of such widely diverse species as bears, tigers, pheasants, and ants. Each of these species has its own early warning system, alerting them in advance of seismic action.

Scientists in the United States now firmly believe that animal behavior before an earthquake must be carefully factored into any early warning system we might devise. Obviously, science writer and editor Fred Warshofsky was right on the money when he wrote, "Nature, through calamity, controls human destiny."

Another clue to the future (and a source of concern to us) is the world's shifting weather pattern.

In May 1977, at a seminar of the Young Presidents Organization, a group to which Dick belongs, I heard the world-renowned climatologist, Dr. Iben Browning, describe some of the consequences of our changing weather scene:

1. Canada will lose forty days out of the growing season in the next twenty years which will take the heart out of the wheat business, and make them importers instead of exporters. (Their spring is later and fall is earlier.)
2. Western Europe will be getting colder for the next 400 years.
3. U.S.S.R. will probably not be able to feed itself for the next one hundred years.
4. China: disastrous drought now; wheat crop failing on top of last year's volcano. May be famine in the next few years in which 10 to 50 million people die.
5. Poland suffered its worst crop failure in history (grain).

6. India: the monsoon failures should not start until around 1983, at which time one-third loss of crops may cause as many as one-quarter of the population to die of starvation.
7. Central America will have drought and locust plagues.
8. Northern Europe will have extreme drought and early frosts.
9. Overall prediction: 50 percent of the world's farmers will go bankrupt.

Dr. Browning went on to say that the tidal forces of the northern hemisphere are rising, so we now have declining temperatures and increasing volcanic activity. These tidal forces will continue to rise for another fifty years, causing the northern hemisphere to get colder. Variable weather is dangerous weather, because so many things—plants, animals, human beings—cannot survive.

Climatological studies show that the last 5,000 years was the warmest period in the last 100,000 years. There are clear signs that this warm period is coming to an end. A 1974 C.I.A. report from the Office of Political Research stated that our entire agricultural science is based on the kind of weather we have had over the past thirty years. It also pointed out that the last thirty years has been a very unusual period of good growing weather, the best since the Middle Ages! A report currently before the World Meteorological Organization links the prolonged droughts in Africa and India and the poor crops in Russia and China to an impending "worldwide climate change."

Why the dramatic shift in our weather patterns? Part of the answer may lie in the increased activity of volcanoes. Within the last decade, major volcanic eruptions have been reported in Antarctica, Chile, Peru, the Galápagos Islands, El Salvador, Costa Rica, Nicaragua, Guatemala, St. Vincent, the West Indies, Alaska, Greenland, Iceland, the Canary Islands, Hawaii, New Zealand, the South Pacific, the Philippines, Indonesia, Japan, the U.S.S.R., Sicily, and Ethiopia. These volcanic eruptions spew vast quantities of dust into the atmosphere, blocking the light of the Sun and thereby causing climatic distortions. The distortions bring a general cooling to the Earth and have been known to cause large areas of drought or flooding. Volcanoes also emit fluorocarbons which may result in the loss of up to 50 percent of our sunlight in the next ten years. Another equally ominous fact: of the roughly 10,000 volcanoes on Earth, 8,500 are located on the edges of continental plates.

In May 1980, Mount St. Helens in Washington state erupted twice, blasting away 1,300 feet of its north slope in a massive explosion that flung hot ash, gases, molten lava, and debris 60,000–80,000 feet into the sky. Scientists calculated the force of the eruption as equal in megatons of TNT to the mightiest H-bomb yet exploded by man. The ash plus sulfuric acid in the upper stratosphere could cause very dramatic weather changes across the grain-growing belts of North America and throughout other parts of the world as well. Here was a part of the Scenario paraded out in living color for all to see.

It could be the tip of the iceberg, since Mount St. Helens is part of the Cascade range, which includes fifteen major volcanoes and stretches about 700 miles from Mount Garibaldi in British Columbia to Lassen Peak in northern California. This strip is the American portion of a circle of volcanoes that rims the Pacific Ocean through South America, Japan, and the Aleutians. Volcanologists call it the "Ring of Fire."

In addition to the molten lava they spew forth, volcanoes precipitate tidal waves, mud slides, and other catastrophes that damage life-support systems and destroy human lives. These kinds of chain reactions are typical of Nature's processes, as this description from the fifteenth edition of the *Encyclopaedia Britannica* demonstrates:

An eruption of Tamboro, Indonesia, took place in 1875. Twelve thousand people lost their lives. The devastation that followed brought famine, and 80,000 people fell victim in the neighboring islands of Sumbawa and Lombok.

In 1883, the volcano Krakatoa in the Malaysian Islands exploded with extreme violence. A resulting sea wave submerged the coastal regions of the neighboring islands of Java and Sumatra and 36,000 people lost their lives.

In September 1979, the following UPI release was picked up by one of the New York papers. The headline read TIDAL WAVE OF DEATH.

Jakarta, Indonesia. Tidal waves triggered by the world's strongest earthquake in two years smashed into a remote Indonesian island, killing scores of people and wreaking widespread destruction, officials said yesterday.

One unofficial report said about 100 people on the tiny island of Yapen were killed by the waves Wednesday. Officials in Jayapura, provincial capital of West Irian, said the tidal waves destroyed at least 400 houses on the east coast of Yapen and left 8,000 people homeless.

There are pieces of the puzzle everywhere I look. Earthquakes, climatic changes, and volcanic eruptions all point to the same conclusion—change, dramatic change. Most scientists and researchers do not connect the changes they outline to the changes described by other disciplines. In addition, the time periods for the changes are almost always ignored. Historically, people resist change at all cost. Unlike members of the animal kingdom who instinctively flee danger, man invariably manages to cling to the illusion of security rather than upset his status quo.

Perhaps no one is willing to take a close look at Earth's predicament. But Dick and I did, and after studying the situation carefully and sifting the available scientific evidence, we became convinced that the Scenario for change was all too valid.

Since man began atomic testing over thirty years ago, the number of earthquakes has increased *over* 400 percent. I have no trouble understanding the cause and effect relationship here. The atomic explosions set off vibrations that are conducted to the core of the Earth. These vibrations then cause additional strain within the Earth's interior as they seek release. The result can be explained by the weakest-link theory: the vibrations seek the most expedient route of escape which is, of course, at the fault or plate lines. Thus earthquakes ensue.

The world's earthquake activity is currently monitored by hundreds of seismic stations as scientists seek to learn the secrets of our changing planet. But it is man himself who holds the key to many of these secrets.

Some of the information we collected about the destiny of our planet coincided with conversations that we later held with the Ogatta group. As we got further into the work, Dick could not resist asking the ETI about the changes that were going to occur. Here are some of the answers he received:

You will be looking at a completely different world in the coming decade. How long is that? Nothing!

And, another time:

There is going to be a shift, a change in the look of things. This is why I stress the need for things to be grown which do not require refrigeration for preservation. No need for electricity, wires, and so forth. Why do you think that telepathy is so vital now? Clairvoyance and clairaudial abilities? Because this is the way you will have to communicate when media is cut off. Mental radio will be the means for communication. When one *cannot* hide anything, honesty will prevail.

When the Tangshan quake was finally reported in our newspapers in 1977, more than a year after its occurrence, the ETI gave the following replies to some of Dick's questions:

I don't know why they just put this in your papers today. It happened thirteen moons ago.

It is a quake that is well brought to the attention of your part of the world. It won't be that long that you are going to have a . . . a . . . do you say a "beaut" . . . in this part of the world.

And finally, in response to pointed and direct questions relating to our family or close friends:

There is a law and order. I wish I could give you a definitive answer. I can but tell you to prepare. You can never know how much I would love to roll that Destiny Screen and tell you, but that is not our way. I will give you direction but not directives.

All these replies further convinced us there is good reason to be aware of the coming changes and to prepare as best we can, each in his own way.

In the summer of 1980, President Carter released a report prepared by the State Department and the Council on Environmental Quality that spoke directly of "man's inhumanity to man." The report concluded with the statement, "If present trends continue, the world in 2000 will be more crowded, more polluted, less stable ecologically, and more vulnerable to disruption than the world we live in now."

Tauri has repeatedly told us that global changes would be due to "man's inhumanity to man—and Nature's plan." Our research pointed very strongly to the part to be played by "Nature's plan."

13

History Repeats Itself

HISTORY repeats itself—monotonously. Since the beginning of time, any number of ages and civilizations have been brought to an abrupt end by violent natural change. The Earth has been called upon to make geological adjustments.

New ages are ushered in every 2,200 to 2,500 years, and the changes are brought about by the altered forces that keep our solar system in orbit on its journey through the Milky Way galaxy. These forces vary, as do the stresses and strains, the frequencies and vibrations that reach our planet; and they interact with every particle of matter, every atom and molecule which make up life and breath on Earth.

There appears to be ample available data to confirm that this is not a new process in the evolution of the Earth. Sources as varied as the Bible, tribal law, and modern science reveal that catastrophes have been an integral part of Earth's development.

Ancient Etruria had records of seven elapsed ages. The Bhagavata Purana, the sacred Hindu book, tells of four, with the current one being the fifth. Buddhists' sacred books refer to seven solar ages. Mazdaism, the ancient religion of the Persians (whose chief prophet was Zoroaster), talks of seven world ages. The Chinese count ten Kis—their term for perished ages—from the "beginning of the world to the age of Confucius."

In the Pacific, Polynesia and Hawaii have traditions of nine different creations and catastrophes. During each period, it was said, there was a different sky above the Earth. In the Americas, cosmic catastrophes can be found in the Mayan and Aztec traditions and inscriptions; their legends describe in great detail a succession of upheavals that decimated humankind and changed the face of the Earth. In the New Testament, first verse, twenty-first chapter of Revelations says,

"Then I saw a new heaven and a new earth, for the first heaven and the first earth had passed away. The sea was no more."

The great philosopher Philo described those "perishing by deluge and consumed by conflagration." He indicates that new conditions were created after each of the catastrophes. The Talmud (Midrash) tells us there were several worlds before ours and all were destroyed. "Ancient traditions know of 'periodic collapse' of the firmament, one of which occurred in the days of the Deluge and which repeated itself at intervals of 1,656 years." Isaiah 65:17 says of God in one sentence: "Behold I shall create new heavens and a new earth and all former things shall not be remembered."

In his book, *Worlds in Collision*, the noted scientist, Immanual Velikovsky, talked about all the catastrophes that repeatedly reduced civilizations on Earth to ruins. These major upheavals displaced the borders of the seas, caused seabeds and continents to change places, submerged kingdoms and created land masses for new ones. Dr. Velikovsky's extensive research clearly indicates that the upcoming natural disasters are anything but unique. They are one more in the long series of inevitable changes that have been metamorphosing Planet Earth since the beginning of time.

Looking to the future, one can only conclude that similar changes are, quite simply, meant to be. Not too long ago, Dick and I were on a Philippine Air Lines flight between Manila and Guam, when my Destiny Screen unexpectedly became activated, and I saw a vast tidal wave emerging from the sea. By chance, Dick had his tape recorder in his flight bag and was able to tape my responses to what I saw.

GRETA: The only ones who will know in advance of the *tidal wave* are the dogs, and then it will be too late.
DICK: Where will this tidal wave be?
GRETA: Sea level.
DICK: Which coast will it hit first?
GRETA: I can't say. It wouldn't be fair.

(Although I had some strong indications of the location, the only one I can, in good conscience, reveal is that it is a place that has more than its share of stray dogs—as my next remarks indicate.)

GRETA: There's no reason for those scraggly dogs to exist, eating what they do, scrounging as they must. As pets, they're ignored. The attention goes to the young people—the children and the infants—not to the animals. *But the dogs will know . . . the dogs will know . . . the dogs will know.*

It isn't surprising that the dogs will know. Like all animals, dogs are extremely sensitive to subtle environmental changes. They would have no trouble detecting the ocean floor vibrations of an impending tidal wave long before the sound waves are within the range of human hearing.

The tidal wave that appeared on my Destiny Screen will dramatically alter the face of Planet Earth. In Iceland, the people talk about their *Edda,* which says that nine worlds went down in a succession of ages due to shifting land masses, rapid changes, tidal waves, and the like. It was in Iceland that I first learned the astounding story of the mammoths. Their fate illustrates the rapidity of climatic shifts of land mass better than anything else I have heard.

The mammoths belonged to a family of prehistoric elephants of northeast Siberia. They—along with the other animals who once inhabited this area and the planet life that once flourished there—no longer exist. The climate changed instantaneously some 10,000–12,000 years ago, and all the animal and plant life perished.

In 1799, the frozen bodies of the mammoths were found intact! Georges Cuvier (1769–1832), the Frenchman who founded the science of vertebrate paleontology (the study of extinct animals), wrote that "their flesh was fibrous and marbled with fat and looked as fresh as well-frozen beef." His fantastic report of their extinction included these facts:

1. If they had not been frozen as *soon* as killed, they would have been decomposed by the putrefaction.
2. They could not have lived in the temperature of eternal frost and therefore it is concluded that the frost could not have previously occupied the area.
3. "It was at one and the same moment" that these animals were destroyed and the country which they inhabited covered with ice.
4. The event was sudden—instantaneous—without *any* gradation.
5. In their stomachs and between their teeth *ingested* grass and leaves were found. The leaves and grass could not grow any closer than 1,000 or more miles away today.
6. Tusks of mammoths were washed up after storms on the shores of

Arctic islands. This shows that part of the land where they lived and were drowned is covered now by the Arctic Ocean.

An article on the front page of the Science section of *The New York Times* for March 4, 1980, told about the Russians' efforts to recreate a live specimen of the mammoth. According to the article, at least five Soviet cytologists—specialists in the reproduction of cells —are working on a project to isolate living cells from a frozen mammoth found in Siberia. Eventually they hope to use them to bring the beasts back after 10,000 years of extinction!

The mammoths are not the only species to vanish so abruptly. Parts of northern Siberia, Alaska, and Canada have islands which appear to be made of bones. Charles Berlitz explains the reason for this in his book, *The Bermuda Triangle:*

[They are] so covered with bones of great animals that suddenly perished (at a date estimated from 10,000 to 11,000 years ago), that some islands or high points where they went for refuge seem to be made entirely of their bones. Other survival points where completely different and inimical species fled for shelter and died in great multitudes have been found across Northern Europe, Central Asia, and China, as if the whole top of the world had experienced a rapid and unexplained climate change at the same time. However, in other hemispheres as well, there are indications of the simultaneous decimation of species, from the huge elephant graveyard that exists in the Colombian Andes, and even under water, as in the case of an enormous sea elephant graveyard off the coast of Georgia. None of these animals had their natural habitats in the places where they met their deaths in such numbers in the sudden climatic change of 12,000 years ago.

Can you visualize waking up tomorrow morning and finding Greenland green? If something like this were to occur, the flooding from the melting icecaps in the Arctic region would raise the levels of the oceans around the world and cause the land masses to shift and change. That sounds ominously like our Scenario and it is entirely possible. How? *Geomagnetic reversals . . . polar flips.*

According to Dr. Velikovsky, the ancient writings indicate a period in our Earth's history when "the sun rose in the west and set in the east." Hugh Auchincloss Brown, engineer and author, is of the opinion that "there have been fearful reverses in the earth's history. . . ." Perhaps another age of change in the magnetic situation is developing, with occasional magnetic earthquake indications as prior warnings.

Drill cores of rock strata from sites around the world all show that the Earth's magnetism has changed direction completely many times—north and south magnetic poles have "flipped," replacing one another. The *Encyclopaedia Britannica* notes:

The ocean floor of the Atlantic consists of progressively older rocks farther from the Mid-Atlantic Ridge, the locus of new crystal generation. Roughly symmetrical bands of rock of alternating magnetic polarity occur on each side of the ridge, and the absolute ages obtained clearly indicate the occurrence of geomagnetic reversals during the time of formation of the ocean floor.

A polar flip can cause climatic conditions to shift so quickly and dramatically that entire species are knocked out in the process. Over the past 2,500 years, the total magnetic field of the Earth has weakened by about 50 percent, leading some experts to believe that a new reversal is inevitable. NASA scientists confirmed, from preliminary results from the downed magnetic field satellite, this previously detected decrease in the intensity of the Earth's magnetic field.

A rapid rise in temperature, such as our hypothetical situation in the Arctic region, could melt all—or a good part of—the icecaps, causing the oceans to rise. The rising waters would in turn cause extensive flooding. Remember Noah and his ark? Almost all the world's races and tribes preserve a vivid account of the Flood. In most cases only a single survivor, along with his family and selected animals, was spared to start a new life. Here are a few examples documenting the flood in prehistory:

1. Noah . . . in the Judeo-Christian tradition.
2. Baisbasbata . . . the flood survivor of the Mahabharata of India.
3. Ut-Napishtim . . . of Babylonian legend, whose story closely resembles that of Noah.
4. Coxcox . . . of ancient Mexico, who escaped the flood in a giant raft.
5. Tezpi . . . of another more developed Mexican race, who had a more spacious vessel at his disposal, on which he loaded grains and animals.
6. Bochica . . . of Colombian Chibcha legend, who finally got rid of the floodwaters by "opening a hole in the earth" (as did the Greek Deucalion).

7. Man of Shuruppak . . . is the Noah of the literaure of the Sumerians.
8. Tamandere . . . of southeastern South America, floated on a huge tree to the top of a mountain, where he survived the deluge.
9. Ziusudra . . . survived the Great Flood of the Mesopotamian account.

It is evident that these myths and sacred histories conform to identical cosmological patterns.

Various geologists note that the level of the oceans at the time that the Third Glaciation started to melt, approximately 10,000–12,000 years ago, was 600 or more feet below its present level. The melting ice caused enormous changes in the land masses. In the Bahamas, underwater discoveries of walls, roads, and remains of structures indicate that thousands of square miles were submerged during this period. Captain Don Henry, an underseas researcher, found a pyramid in the Atlantic Ocean in what has become known as the Bermuda Triangle. Pyramids go back to that period of prehistory when the monuments were designed with proportions that are the same worldwide, and which are founded on principles and information that are something of a mystery, even today.

Henry traced the size and shape of the Atlantic pyramid with modern sonar equipment, and the tracings were corroborated by Dr. Manson Valentine of the Museum of Science in Miami, Florida, and a sonar expert named J. M. Pirtle. The statistics from the tracings showed the following:

1. Location—50 miles off South Florida where sea bottom is almost perfectly flat between South Bimini Island and the north end of Cay Sal Bank.
2. Submerged in 1,200 feet of water.
3. Rises steeply to great height of 780 feet (the tallest known pyramid is Cheops, which is 481 feet high).
4. Base measurements are 1,000 feet on each side.

The discoveries off the coast of Florida are not unique. Other submerged land masses appear at one time to have bridged Siberia and Alaska, Sicily and Italy, and Africa with Gibraltar. Georges Cuvier believed that the land and sea had exchanged places many times in the history of the planet. Studies of his native country showed that France was once sea; then it was land populated by land reptiles; then it became sea again and was populated by marine animals; then it was land again inhabited by mammals; then it was once more sea . . . and then again land. Each layer or strata of the Earth that Cuvier studied contained the evidence of its age in the bones and shells of the animals that lived during the period, and were entombed in the recurrent upheavals. However, the scientist never found any satisfactory theory or explanation of why these changes occurred.

I return to a few random channeled thoughts from our ETI friends:

T: Due to man's inhumanity to man and Nature's plan, there will be a change to the face of your planet. Nature's holocaustic endeavor to cleanse Planet Earth in the way she knows best.

and

T: View the change not with fear but with the calm knowledge of what is to come. And be ready for it.

and

T: There will be floods, fire, famine, hurricanes, tidal waves. . . .

and

T: As the Sun reaps its own holocaust, so it sends back its beams to heal. Same to be said for Moon.

Whenever I am tempted to brood about the destruction and changes that are in store for all of us here on Planet Earth, my conversations with the ETI sustain me. I think especially of Tauri's message that "calm knowledge" will overcome our fears and prepare us for what is to come. I think about a more highly energized planet which will have a brighter future etched onto its altered face after "what is to come" has turned into past history. My family and I plan to prepare for it—live through it—and be survivors who will face new and different horizons.

14

Badinage

"CONQUER FEAR, you conquer failure," Tauri told us.

From the first days of ETI's entering our lives, they wanted us to trust them, to believe in their capacity to understand and identify with all aspects of our human nature. Above all, they did not want us to think of them in any way as awesome, despite their advanced technologies and evolvement. (On a scale of 0 to 10, they place us on Planet Earth at around 2 while nonchalantly rating themselves at about 7.)

The ETI have always offered us friendship and hope to receive ours in return. They want our cooperation, and over the years have come to realize that they can depend upon it in the difficult years to come. What they do not want—but get—is our unflagging gratitude and sense of wonderment—particularly when they play games and perform feats for our amusement and/or benefit.

Some of their activities have been so utterly hilarious, outrageous, staggering to the imagination, that I want to share them with you. Where to begin? How about the day we were en route to New Hampshire and Tauri was sharing the channel?

T: In the beginning when I'd visit, I'd say "I got here!" and you'd laugh and wonder what kind of "cosmic showbiz" will happen now? Well, it was very important that we play the games for you, because interspersed in the funnies were bits and pieces of serious things that *did* come to pass. It was an easy way to prepare you for the real work in the future. All things tie together.

D: Can you do something, Tauri, that ties in to nothing—just to "bobble my mind" as you call it? We used to have such a good time when you defied our natural laws.

94

T: Ohhh, my goodness. You want fun and games, do you, my dear Dick? Well. Look up at the sky. What do you see?

D: Nothing. I don't see anything.

T: No clouds at all?

D: No. No clouds. Nothing.

T: Look again, but be careful when you drive your wondrous machine. Look straight ahead.

(Greta's hand moved up slowly and waved across the windshield.)

D: Good grief! Can anyone *else* see it?

T: Yes, and they'll think "Oh, that looks *just* like letters in the sky!" Now look again, for they will go away quickly, quickly.

D: Tauri, you're too much. I'm always amazed at the things you can do!

(Spelled out in perfectly formed block letters about two feet high was the word OGATTA which stretched across the expanse of sky. It appeared to be made of clouds.)

This was not the first time that Tauri had used the skies for demonstrations that left us speechless. On an earlier occasion we were with Andrija Puharich's Space Kids at the Mind Link—a gathering of his dedicated group for the express purpose of driving a unified shaft of energy, a slide of light, to a higher dimension. A beautiful young woman felt unworthy to be part of the group because she did not know what her "mission" was to be. Tauri showed herself to the bewildered Susan and suggested that she walk into the woods with her. Dick stayed at my right side and Susan stayed at my left, as we walked into the clearing indicated.

T: If you ride the merry-go-round and you reach for the brass ring, and you catch it, that's fine. If you ride the merry-go-round and you reach for the brass ring, and you miss it, don't let your music stop, because, remember, merry-go-rounds come round again and you have another chance at the ring.

Then Tauri instructed Susan to stand still and look up at the one open patch of sky directly overhead in an otherwise cloudy night.

T: Look straight up and tell me, how many stars do you see in that one clearing?

S: I see four.

T: I am going to show you how my energy can move clouds. [TAURI *snapped* GRETA's *fingers above her eyes.*] How many stars do you see now?

S: *Six!*

T: How many now? [*Snap-snap.*]

S: *Eight!*

T: Ah. So, you saw a wondrous thing, did you? Now, is it enough that I feel you have every right to be here? I tell you for your own head, do not worry about being dropped from the group and do not worry about staying and being incapable of contributing. You have not had the experiences of my channel but you are right to be here with your sensitivities. Yes. I say it is a good thing you be here, child with the beautiful eyes. Now, look at the sky [*snap-snap*] and what do you see?

S: Ohh. Back to only four stars. How . . . how did you do that? Thank you. . . .

Tauri was to move clouds on three other occasions, once for a medical student who needed "impressing" on the subject of the absolute existence of ETI. Later, Dick, who was always there, would describe the episodes to me or to the children. His accounts were unfailingly lively, but the person for whom the act was executed was also interesting to listen to. He or she would stammer and splutter in excitement. "How did she do it? How? *Wow!*"

I considered that progress because they were never asked "How do *you* do it? They accepted ETI, knowing full well that *I* was totally incapable of producing such wonders.

Half the fun of ETI dialogues is in the actual *hearing* of the interchanges. Tauri, especially, has a most endearing and smile-filled husky whisper of a voice which rises and falls with outrageous cadences. When excited, she fairly stammers out a rat-a-tat-tat spate of words: "You-you-you strange hyoooman being, you!" (Jonathan does the best imitation in our family of her inimitable lilt and inflection.)

I learned about my parent civilization on Ogatta, but I was not told about any of my prior experiences. Dick, on the other hand, knew nothing at all about his past, or if indeed he had a home civilization outside Planet Earth. He constantly tried to josh the Ogatta group into telling him something, anything. One episode still has us giggling. It began with his lighthearted conjecturing to Tauri, "I'll bet I'm from Ogatta." "Was I once a knight?" "Maybe I'm Henry the

VIII reincarnated!" "Is there a chance that I could have been Plato?"

Tauri always ignored such queries, until one night she caught Dick unawares by asking, "And just who do you think you are tonight, dear Dick?"

He retorted, "Oh, maybe I'm Martin Luther King!"

Without a pause Tauri came right back with, "No. Impossible. You are married to GRRRRReta, not CORetta."

Those ETI know everything!

We have also been intrigued by how much they enjoy entertaining us with their quips and tricks. Listen to this exchange between Tauri and Dick:

T: It's a funny to tease you, Dick.

D: You are a master of badinage.

T: Badinage? Another word in your lingo? What is badinage?

D: Oh, it means teasing, a sort of light bantering back and forth.

T: Well, I'm not teasing when I tell you I must leave you now. Be with my channel. Your love is the acknowledged source of her strength. And Dick . . .

D: Yes, Tauri?

T: I enjoyed badinaging with you!

The last episode of cloud-moving occurred on the night of August 9, 1980. Two young Philadelphians were spending the weekend at our home for the express purpose of further developing their unique extrasensory abilities. A little before midnight we grabbed quilts, pillows, and some munchies, and went outside onto a back lawn to view the meteorite showers that had been predicted in all the media. Clouds were heavy in the northeast section of the sky, the particular area where the celestial fireworks were anticipated to be most visible. Our daughter Ann suggested that I try to move the offending clouds away and I agreed that it would be fun to try. Four minutes later, there was not a single cloud to be seen in the patch of star-studded heaven to which my guests had pointed. We all watched those clouds literally dissolve, to the bubbling excitement of our young friends (and to Dick and Ann and me). "Where'd they go?" "Look at that one break up!" "Oh, gee, who will ever believe this?" I never kidded myself that *I* had done it, despite the insistence of members of the Ogatta group that such was the case on that delicious night.

One of our most hilarious encounters with the Ogatta group took place in 1977 at Trader Vic's in the elegant Plaza Hotel in New York City. Dick, Jill, and Jonathan are all July babies, and we four were celebrating their combined birthdays by going out to dinner, and then on to see *The King and I* on Broadway. Suddenly into the restaurant came Zeoker, one of our Planet Archa ETI who never need words to make their messages clear as crystal. Greeting us all with identifiable nods, bows, and smiles, Zeoker, using me as his channel, leaned across the table, hands stretched palms upward (mine) and out of nowhere, a *huge* green tea leaf appeared on his open hands. He smiled at Jonathan and handed it to Jill, who seized it as if she feared it would disappear as fast as it had appeared, dematerialize as it had materialized. Perhaps to tease us still further, Zeoker had chosen a moment to present his leafy gift when three persons were being escorted to their table—next to ours. All three of them stopped dead in their tracks to watch "magic."

Soon after that, Omee, with her high, lilting, smiling voice (way above the range of my natural voice chords), arrived at our table. She wished both our J's a happy birthday and dispensed the delightfully scented firna to Dick. Tauri came in and huskily sent her greetings to the three celebrants and said she hoped everyone would enjoy the music of the show we were about to see a few blocks away.

We left the restaurant, Jill with shining eyes, clutching the twenty-three-inch-long tea leaf, Jonathan looking miffed. I turn to Dick's notes, classics in themselves:

Jonathan elbowed me to look at Greta, who was obviously being used as a channel again, because she was waddling down Broadway in the typical Archan walk. Her features were radically changed and "she" was definitely now a "he." None of us recognized his face. It wasn't our friend Zeoker nor was it Bilakka. He stared hard at Jill, who asked him if he knew what kind of a leaf she held. He reached out, grasped the leaf in two hands like a cob of corn, and in the manner of a beaver, ate straight across the entire leaf, his teeth rat-a-tatting with lightning speed. He smiled, indicated that it was not "one of his" and handed it back with its nibbled marks all across one long side.

Later, when Dick, Jill, and Jonathan told me about the episode, I had to laugh, visualizing all these people walking around the theater district and seeing a strange creature chomping and swallowing a gigantic leaf. I was even more amused by what followed. The entity was apparently prepared to keep walking straight ahead, despite red lights or cars. Jonathan and Dick grabbed me on either side and, according to the notes, the visitor happily marched between them, or more accurately, waddled, looking quizzically and brightly about.

When we all entered the beautiful Uris Theater, our visitor stepped onto the escalator in the lobby, reached with interest for the red hair of the woman on the moving step above him, and began stroking it with obvious satisfaction and delight. She, I am told, turned around, and saw a middle-aged woman with a birdlike scrunchy male face stroking, and not letting go, of her hair. No one ever told me this, but I strongly suspect one of my birthday darlings told her I was demented, but harmless.

Let Dick's transcript tell you what happened next:

Quickly, we managed to get the channel to her seat, which happened to be front row, orchestra. Our new friend looked around in satisfaction and showed no intention of leaving. Where was Greta? Suddenly, a friend of Jonathan and Jill's from Princeton was seen by Jonathan, coming down the aisle, straight toward us. Jonathan took one last look at Greta and leaped over her seat to get out of the row before the friend could come over. How would one explain the nonspeaking, bright-eyed entity to a girl who was Summa Cum Laude, Phi Beta Kappa, Marshall Scholar, Pyne Prize Winner, and an accepted candidate to Harvard Medical School? No way! While he was marching a perplexed girl back up the aisle, I (Dick) tried to establish the identity of our new friend! He motioned for a writing instrument and wrote onto the program in left-handed different-looking characters, "They like him very much." He then pointed to the name Richard Rodgers inside the *Playbill*, folded his arms, and settled back in Greta's expensive seat to enjoy the overture. Seconds before the music began, Jonathan returned to his seat a bit breathless, saw the odd message and asked if he could have it since Jill had the leaf. The entity smiled but shook his head negatively and carefully folded it into a perfect square and placed it between Greta's right thumb and forefinger. The overture began and ended, and everyone applauded the familiar music. The entity looked around, and to be part of the action, raised his arms straight up over his head (directly in front of the orchestra leader's face as he was about-faced for his bows) and clapped in the way a seal would flip his flippers. The kids were convulsed when the lights went down, the curtain went up, and Greta said, "What happened to the overture? Hey, why no overture?" She looked at her hand holding the wadded square of paper and said, "Gee, I am tempted to hide this paper . . ." when poof! it was gone. As the King (Yul Brynner) sang later, " 'Tis a puzzlement." Before the second act, Tauri came through to whisper that Dryzek was pleased to have visited and been part of the party celebration, and that he "knows all about Shubert Alley and the area." She stayed to hear Anna (Constance Tower) sing a solo.

So our new friend was named Dryzek? Yes. Did I see much of the show? No. At this writing, Jill still has her leaf—dried out, brown, brittle, and tooth-marked. Jonathan has his memories of maneuvering an entity down one aisle and a friend up another. And Dick mumbles to himself whenever I play the tape of the *King and I*, but he mumbles happily.

Dick was far from mumbling a year before when he had his very own cosmic birthday party. He takes pride in his garden, and plants enough vegetables and flowers to supply half the county. The one thing he looks forward to most, however, is the tomato season when he can harvest the acid-free yellow tomatoes that he particularly enjoys. In 1977, he had been late in buying and could not find any plants or seeds of this variety. It was obviously going to be a summer in which he would have to forego his small indulgence.

Dick's birthday found him out in the garden pruning, and when he looked up, there was Zeoker studying his crops. Zeoker corrected Dick's pruning method and then stepped over to examine the tomato plants. Through a charade method of communication, Dick explained his disappointment at not having any acid-free tomatoes. Zeoker, in response, made it infinitely clear that Dick could eat as many regular tomatoes as he liked without fear of excess acidity because he, Zeoker, would make them acid-free as a birthday gift.

Tauri came in to remark, "My dear Dick, he wants to give you a present on your day of being. It might be fun for you to get those papers to test yourself." (She meant litmus papers which are used to measure the acid in the system. The papers are naturally pink, but when immersed in urine, they turn blue if the solution is alkali and red if it is acid.)

Dick tested. Acid-free. He was able to indulge himself without any ill effects all through the August and September harvests; he was, indeed, eating "forbidden fruit."

Not to be outdone, some others from the Ogatta group came to see my Dear Ezra. Omee—who told him all about the various birds with whom she works. The stilvahs (who talk like mynah birds but have the long legs of storks), kitzbers (who look like little doves), chinkers (much like our cardinals), redewers (who hunt for the other birds), balangeries (ostrichlike and scatterbrained).

Omee asked Dick if he would like to see one of the birds for his birthday and he nodded in great excitement. "A stilvah, then," and in a wink, above the garden enclosure "hung" a silly-looking bird with long flamingolike legs. In a pine tree close by sat a second one staring straight at Dick. "Happy birthday, Dick," and both birds vanished.

Dick stood rooted to the ground and stared into empty space. He was taken out of his reverie when another of the ETI, Cjork, came by to give him a liberal sprinkling of firna and "a vibration and heat" that stayed with him all day. Dick's arm had been throbbing due to a fall, and she healed it (permanently). A knowing smile, and Cjork was gone, but little Tauri returned and told him to "Look into the eyes of my channel so that you may see beyond them." What Dick saw is not recorded.

Badinage: *noun. "Light banter."*

We were planning a trip to Australia with the Young Presidents Organization in April 1978. A post-seminar around the Pacific Rim was under consideration; it was to be led by a member named Sheldon Woolf, whom we did not know. We assumed that Woolf was a member of the Australian chapter, but his name was not in the 1977 directory which we had at home. We therefore concluded he had to be a new member of Y.P.O. and that his name would definitely be in the 1978 directory which was in Dick's New York office. I remarked that I'd like to talk to Sheldon Woolf to see what sort of seminar he was planning before sending in our deposit and committing ourselves to make the trip. Dick promised to look up Mr. Woolf at the office the next day. Enter Tauri:

T: My channel is a game player. Tell her to think about the Second Law of Motion. Or the First Law of Motion. *Then* think about your **Mr. Woolf.**

She popped out as quickly as she came in. Dick repeated the re-mark, and we concluded that it had something to do with transporta-tion and travel plans. I asked Dick to explain the laws of motion to me and he began by noting that Isaac Newton wrote them. Suddenly, Dick the non-game-player remarked, "Well, the only other Newton that comes to mind is the place Newton, Massachusetts, but that doesn't mean anything." I immediately went to the phone, dialed in-formation for the area code of Newton, Massachusetts, and asked for the telephone number of Mr. Sheldon Woolf. There *was* such a list-ing and we called and talked to the man who was indeed leading the seminar. We subsequently took the trip, feeling it was meant to be—although we never told Shelley how we found him until February 1980, when we met again in Orlando, Florida. Well, he heard the words . . .

Fun-happenings à la ETI. On February 6, 1978, I was listening to the local weather report at 10 A.M. The forecast: "Winds from the northwest and gales up to forty miles-per-hour. Winds expected to turn to the southwest by nighttime."

I turned to a friend who was staying with us and remarked—in complete contradiction to the forecast—"It's going to be a nor'-easter."

Throughout the day we listened to the reports, and each time I'd shake my head and say, "No. It's going to be a nor'easter." My friend wondered why I kept saying that, knowing as I did that my sense of direction is about as good as my ability to bake yak pie. At 5:50 P.M. the newscaster reported, "Winds have shifted strangely, and we may be in for a nor'easter, so batten down the hatches." My guest stayed over for another night rather than travel in such wretched weather.

When I finally settled down to write this book, I had a secret hope that it would be "channeled." I had grandiose visions of sitting at the typewriter with my fingers flying over the keys as all kinds of marvelous information poured out onto the pages. I know one person who channels that way, but I was not so lucky.

As Tauri said too many times, "All the information you need is right there, so write it. Why else would our Dear Ezra have taken all those notes?" Only twice have the ETI even commented on the book once I had agreed to write it. The first time was a casual remark about the Cosmos, "That's a capital 'C,' you know." (I had been spelling it in lowercase.) The second intervention was much less casual. It began with the title of this book, which was *Dear Ezra.*

I loved that title. Not only would I dedicate my effort to my husband, but I felt it was appropriate, since without his scribings I would have remembered none of the details and nuances I intended to recount. *Dear Ezra* started to take form, and I cleared half a drawer in my business office filing cabinet, and hung a Pendaflex folder onto the bars. These folders have vertical slits on the top into which you slip plastic tabs with labels inside to show what's in the file. *Dear Ezra* now had a file all its own, but after a few weeks I suddenly noticed that the plastic tab no longer had a label. I was somewhat surprised that it had fallen out; it's always a tight squeeze to get them in. But thinking nothing of it, I took all the papers out of the folder, spotted the tiny label saying *Dear Ezra* on the bottom, and slipped it back into its plastic holder.

That night I locked the filing cabinet. But when I unlocked it the next morning to take out the manuscript, the name was missing again. Again, I thought nothing of it. I found it, replaced it, and finished my day's work. When it was time to lock up and put the manuscript away, however, I saw that for the third time the name was gone. Not gone completely, mind you, just lying on the bottom of the folder. I got the message and laughed out loud. "Ah, so you don't like the title *Dear Ezra?* I do!" And I went to bed. Morning dawned, and no title, not even in the bottom of the folder. It was *gone.*

After due consideration, I typed out a new title, *The Tauri Story,* inserted the label into the plastic tab, and moved the whole file into my desk—which has a special drawer outfitted to hold such files. It stayed there without incident for two days before it, too, fell to the bottom of the file. I knew better than to replace it. Instead, I started thinking about another title and happily came up with *The Ogatta Group.* It lasted a week. I tried *The Coming of the Gattae* which I didn't particularly like, knowing it would be mispronounced (it's gat-eye). My little friends must have agreed, because it was gone in forty-eight hours.

At that point I remembered the time Dick had spent a full nine months looking for a perfect star sapphire for me to wear at my throat, a perfectly formed and dazzling star with its own faceted slide of light. It was to become my exquisite twenty-fifth anniversary gift, which even pleased the Ogatta group.

At the Mind Link with Andrija's Space Kids, Tauri had invited us to "ride on a slide of light." On that occasion, using me as her channel, she had said:

I would like very much to leave you today on a shaft of light so white that it is pearlized, luminous, iridescent. . . .

Tauri went on to tell us other things that I will share with you later in this book, but in urging us to look to the future, she used one expression that aptly described what we would be doing:

Twenty-four-plus civilizations wait and look and say to you to ride that slide of light that you may see for yourselves what was revealed to my channel.

I knew Dick was remembering that message from Tauri when he started searching for my anniversary gift. I recalled his telling me how each time he found a sapphire with brilliant facets in the star, he would "sense" it to be wrong. Finally, he came across one so amazing in its color and movement that even competitive jewelers admitted the stone was unique. My slide of light—and Tauri's. Yes, *On a Slide of Light* as a title appealed to me, if I wasn't permitted to use *Dear Ezra*. As of this moment, the title has stayed in the tab on the folder for better than ten months. If, when you read this book, it has yet another title, know that it probably evolved the way the others did.

15

Persiflage

THOUGHT *impressions* are clean, crisp, and un-muddled when given via the telepathic route. Thought *expressions*, on the other hand, are restricted and limited by words. Perhaps that is why the members of the Ogatta group are fascinated by our language. They have their own universal language for communication when they telepathize, but they are curious about our phraseology and frequently inquire about certain expressions we use. When we explain what they mean, the ETI always get the idea beautifully, but to our great amusement, they will frequently mix up the words.

Is it deliberate? Perhaps. Whatever the reasons, the results are highly entertaining. Once Dick gave me a book which I didn't read, and he took it back. Omee called him a "Sioux-giver" (which took us time to figure out). Another time Omee told one of our kids, "If the slipper fits, wear it." In light chastisement for not following through on a specific study, Tauri "slapped our arms," and on another occasion she cautioned our daughter Ann not to "tale-tattle." Tauri also wondered about "playing leap-toad" and asked why we laughed when we said something was a "scream." And once she declared, "A turkey is a bird. Why do you call *him* a turkey?"

Our family nicknames and pet endearments used to drive all the ETI crazy. Our sons, for instance, call each other "Peach" (which dates back to their first shaving-the-peach-fuzz days). Ann is called "Pooz"—a hangover from her Pooh Bear stage. The two J's refer to each other as "Meus"—which began in high school Latin with *Mea Soror* and *Meus Frater*. Dick is "B.D." or "Big D" for Big Dad.

"Why?" "What does it mean?" the Ogatta group keep asking as they try to latch on to our lingo. "Verrry pe-cyuuuu-liar!"

D: We're just having fun, Tauri . . . a matter of kidding around.
T: A little "badinage"?

D: No, persiflage.

T: Persiflage?

D: Same thing, really. Treating something frivolously.

T: Humans have a very pe-cyuuuliar lingo!

D: Tell me one of your Ogattan words that I'd like.

T: Use your "hoyja."

D: Hoyja? My *mind*?

T: No. It's your, your *intuition*, "B.D."

D: Ah, Tauri, if I don't have hoyja, will you let me call on you?

T: Why Dick, just dial Galaxy 1.618.

D: 1.618? That's the secret to the harmonics Bilakka gave us!

T: I'm so grateful you explained that to me! More important, you explain *it*.

Certain expressions such as "the Ogatta group," "we pick our people well," or "the coming of the gattae" are repeated frequently but not monotonously. Our own idioms are referred to as "your lingo," but there are twists of phrase which are theirs alone and never fail to evoke our smiles:

"a closed-eye experience" (sleep)

"in a few moons" (months)

"it bobbles my mind" (boggles)

"by the tick-tock" (time)

"your coins" (money)

"keep it light" (don't be ponderous)

"the I-go" (ego)

"wondrous machine" (car)

"head noises" (headache)

"know your music"

"I have to go 'out there' "

" a slide of light"

"in a couple of blinks" (which can be days, weeks, or months in our rigidly linear time frame)

While the ETI are amused at our family's pet names, they themselves have nicknamed some of us. Our son Alan, who has deep dimples and a cleft in his chin, is called "the one with holes in his face." Dick is "Dear Ezra," and Jill, with her strawberry blonde hair, is called "the one with bruge hairs." Jonathan has "soulful eyes" and Ann is "the little one." They all refer to me as "my channel" and to Andrija as the "Good Doctor."

One of my expressions, power pack—referring to those who provide extra energy boosts to healers—is now a favorite term of the Ogatta group. It is a concept to which they easily relate and they have amplified my ability to teach "rooting"—a technique for drawing energy from the Earth—to those welcome persons who give of their time and energy to help others. Our ETI have a melodious word for this healing energy—*reisha.*

One of the things we can't help noticing about the Ogatta group is that each entity has his or her own way of announcing a successful arrival. Tauri's explosive, lilting "I *got* here!" is endearing, but my family always recognizes her presence even before the words come out. The delicious aroma of firna which the entities dispense is both unmistakable and unforgettable. Its opposite, pitraeon, is equally unmistakable and unforgettable—only it's horrible. Fortunately, the ETI unleashed it on us only once in a moment of rare pique.

T: So you smelled my pitraeon, did you? You thought it was—what— "blue-cheesey"?

D: Tauri, you are naughty to dispense so horrible an odor in a restaurant!

T: Ah, you are slapping my arms, are you? Well, lest you did not notice, my dear Ezra, *only* you and the two at your table could smell it and nobody else.

D: It certainly was a weird, unpleasant smell.

T: Yes. It is pronounced pit-ree-on and spelled *pitraeon.* I tell you this so you will know for next time.

D: Oh, please don't ever let there be a next time. We all gagged.

T: It came as a reminder for you—be careful of what you reveal and discuss, my dear Dick. [TAURI *then threw out firna.*]

At times other members of the Ogatta group threatened to send pitraeon but they never actually did—thank goodness!

Our adventures with the ETI are never-ending. One evening, Andrija, Dick, and our son, Alan, were sitting in the den when Tauri came through. Dick reminded her of the time she had shown him a tiny kitzber bird in flight when we were in Florida. She chuckled, remembering the contrast she had pointed out between the overworked flappings of a sea gull and the effortless wing-edge flutter of her bird.

Tauri then turned to Andrija and Alan and asked if they would like to have a kitzber feather. When they nodded, she instructed them to find some envelopes and place them in their laps. This done, she next suggested that they look inside the envelopes. They obeyed, and in each envelope found a tiny, fluffy, white feather of indescribable softness. Alan put his on his palm, gazed at it dreamily, then carefully returned it to his envelope and sealed it. After studying his, Andrija observed that it looked more like "manna" than a bird's feather. In a twinkling, there was Tauri, very cosmically ruffled. "Well!" she exclaimed. "If I tell you it is a feather, dear Doctor, I assure you that it is so. And now, so much for your 'manna.' "

In another twinkling she was gone and so was Andrija's feather. Andrija pleaded—into thin air—for her to "please give it back" and confessed that he had made a "terrible mistake," but Tauri never mentioned the incident again.

At that point, Alan nervously tore open his envelope and found that his feather had also disappeared. He told us that he mentally begged Tauri to return it since there was no doubt in his mind that it was a kitzber feather. Tauri's next appearance made him happier: "Go, you with the holes in your face (she was ever amused at dimples and cleft chins) and get another envelope."

Alan ran upstairs and came back with a business envelope.

"Is it empty?"

"Yes, Tauri."

"Look again."

He looked and there was another gorgeous little feather inside. Alan cherished it and for a long time kept it hidden even from us.

Our memories of the feather episode were further heightened after the event we came to refer to as our cosmic twenty-fifth anniversary. As an anniversary gift, our four offspring—unbeknownst to us—conceived a plan to have a talented local artist sculpt their interpretation of the entire Ogatta group. The sculpture turned out to be a birdlike bronze statue, complete with sculpted feathers, freestanding on a little base. The arms were spread wide and under the two wings were hands. The eyes, of course, were large, luminous, and humanoid. In a flash of whimsy, the kids had the artist add a wee spaceship to the figure's back. Into this gattae went Alan's precious feather.

Dick and I both adore this gift of gifts and never allow anyone to open the tiny gattae where the feather is ensconced.

During the first weeks after our anniversary, many of our ETI were in and out of the house. They never failed to stop and gaze at the sculpture. We looked for the usual signs of their approval— arms upward, palms up, head back—but they never appeared. Zeoker in particular seemed disturbed about the position of the arms and the angle of the neck on the little bronze statue.

Over the course of the next three months each of us gradually realized the shape of the figure was subtly changing. The neck was arching up and the arms were getting higher. When several of our friends began commenting on the changes, I felt it was time to have the artist—Steffi Friedman—come over and take a look for herself. Steffi had carefully photographed the piece from every angle before consigning it to our children, and it was now a proud addition to her portfolio. I asked her to bring the pictures with her. I can tell you a great deal about her visit that day, but it will be simpler if I let you read the letter which she sent to me in obvious bewilderment.

STEFFI FRIEDMAN   *Sculptor*
9 Yankee Hill Road
Westport, Ct. 06880

Dear Greta,

I designed an imaginative, humanized, upward-striving eagle, arms and hands reaching toward the sky. I incorporated a small spaceship on its back. The sculpture was modeled directly in wax in August 1977. Using the traditional lost wax method it was cast in bronze in September 1977. At the completion of the sculpture, I took photographs of the piece (photo enclosed). The sculpture was then turned over to the four children who had commissioned me to create the piece as a gift from them to their parents. It is prominently displayed in the Woodrew home.

At my recent visit to Greta Woodrew's home, the first thing I noticed was a decided shift in the angle of my eagle bird. The head, neck, and arms had a much sharper upward strive. This piece of sculpture, being solid bronze, could *not* change on its own at any time, yet comparing it to the pictures I had taken, there is a perceptible change.

Greta, you asked me to write down my impressions after reviewing my piece in your home. I thought you might be interested in hearing about my most unusual observation about my own sculpture. Bronze does *not* change shape, but that bird is definitely in a different position. It is beautiful, but altered.

I loved visiting with you, but I am really not sure that I enjoyed this most perplexing happening for which I have *no* explanation at all. Thanks for asking me over.

With best regards,
Steffi

P.S. Hope you'll let me borrow the sculpture for my next Gallery Art Show. I would also be delighted to prominently display your *Ezekiel* bronze which they tell me is "of museum quality." I really am pleased that you and Dick love it.

Our "cosmic twenty-fifth" was full of fascinating surprises, but the highlight occurred at home late on the evening of November 16, 1977. I was wearing the lovely star sapphire that Dick had given me earlier in the day.

T: The slide of light around my channel's throat is lovely, lovely. You chose it well, dear Dick. So I look into the ray of the star. Luminous. Beautiful. Here, we have no need for "things" as you know them, but the slide of light is special and beautiful to commemorate a special and a beautiful occasion. I give you a *"yes!"* [*Ogatta gesture of approval, palms/arms up.*] A few here wish to share your evening. I step aside for Cjork.

c: You knew that I was with you in the Land of Ices, did you not, dear Dick?

This was a reference to the Frontiers of Physics Conference in Reykjavik, Iceland, a few weeks earlier. I'll tell you all about our adventures there later on in this book. Suffice it to say for now that I did some channeling and was able to do some demonstrations for the assembled scientists that amazed them (and me).

D: Oh, Cjork, how I admired your incredible techniques with the baron and the deaf child and the cancer patients.

c: Well, I believe they are all a little better in health for the help, but our channel is still dry from it all. Never mind that now. We are healers first and foremost here on Oshan, as you well know. Healing is our prime function. If I could blush I would blush to think that perhaps you overestimate the knowledge I have—the ability. I come on this perfect end to a perfect day to give you my gift, for you will have great need of strength and good health in the year ahead. While we cannot always safeguard hers, we can at this moment of your quarter-century milestone guarantee yours for twelve moons.

Cjork put her hands on Dick's forehead, moved one hand slowly behind and came down with a thunderous chop on his right collarbone. It did sound and look "killing" but strangely enough, it did not hurt. Rather to the contrary.

D: Thank you, oh, Cjork, thank you. How can you do that? I feel tingling.

C: I leave you in Zeoker's hands.

D: Welcome, Zeoker. My! Thank you for this gorgeous leaf. It's magnificent. [ZEOKER *gestured to smell it.*] Why it smells a bit like mint. Is it from your planet? Yes? Will it live here? No? Well, I thank you for it. Ah, it's for your channel? She is to *eat* it? I'll tell her that you . . . where do you want to go?

(Zeoker jumped up, waddled upstairs to our living room where the Ogatta group sculpture stands, and started admiring the flowers that our friends and relatives had sent us for our anniversary.)

D: Yes, you love the flowers! Which have the nicest vibrations of the ones here, can you show me? Oh, those are lilies. Those are shafts of wheat. Yes, yes, those are iris and roses. [ZEOKER came *to a basket which had a paisley bow with artificial buds in the middle, and he became convulsed with laughter over it.*] Tell me, Zeoker, is it a nice feeling to have so many flowers around? Yes? Oh, you are examining the gift that our children gave us. Does it remind you of the Ogatta group? [ZEOKER *stared long and hard at the eyes and smiled. He motioned the position of the arms and jumped into the pose of the "Yes" gesture, pointing frantically to the bird.*] What is it, Zeoker? It isn't 100 percent right? Well, the artist doesn't know you. Where are you going? [ZEOKER *grasped the bird and moved it across the room to place it on the piano with a light directly overhead. He gave another "Yes" gesture and left the channel, letting* BILAKKA *in.*]

D: Bilakka, how wonderful of you to come here on my anniversary. Will you play an anniversary special tune for us and let me tape it for Greta to hear? Yes? Wait, let me put the tape recorder over here near the piano. [BILAKKA *sat down and played a melody of haunting beauty on the black notes, signaling that the piece was from him to* GRETA *and me.*] I cannot understand you. Please don't get frustrated, try telling me again. Oh, those from Archa like the little bird? [BILAKKA *gave a "Yes," touched the statue and left.*] Smell that firna. Who's here? Is that you, Awis?

O: It's Omee, and I had to come in here one time.

D: I've missed you, Omee. I've missed your exquisite smile and your voice.

o: I have been around you both all evening, yes; but I must use your words of Happy Anniversary to you and my channel because the tick-tock goes by so fast that soon your moments of celebration will technically end. I will not stay and hurt the voice of my channel, but I send you firna. I go quickly, for your guest from Mennon is here, and one doesn't keep Hshames waiting, no.

h: One word with you so that Mennon is represented tonight. Congratulations on your beautiful union. Each hour in your time frame, each day in your week, each week in your month, each month in your year during the *next* quarter century in your time frame—may they glow as brightly as the star you gave our channel. May they stay as burnished as the piece she gave you, and the littler piece the children gave to you both. *Yes.*

t: My dear Dick, this will not be easy to do, but they will try. They want so very badly, so very badly, to be represented from Tchauvi tonight. My channel is still dry. Dry. Get a glass of moisture, some water for her might help. [*Suddenly, from* GRETA's *throat came a Tchauvian chant, different from the one we had heard twice before. There seemed to be many voices joined in song and harmony.*]

d: I thank you, Tchauvians, for such music. Who is here?

t: He's Rynjavi. He brought you a most special chant. You and my channel.

d: I am overwhelmed at all of you coming to talk to us. Why, we heard the entire Ogatta group—Ogatta, Oshan, Mennon, Archa, Tchauvi!

t: Yes, you heard from the entire jorpah.

d: What is a jorpah, Tauri?

t: It's a cosmic grouping.

d: Thank you. Thank you all for coming. What an amazing night and what a fantastic experience and anniversary present, your all coming in to talk to us. All of you beautiful, beautiful beings.

t: I leave you to your human anniversary.

d: You have made it much more beautiful than I could have imagined. Oh, I can't wait to let Greta hear this tape. Or eat this leaf!

t: Let's not push her. [*Snap-snap*] I have ingested it *for* her, dear Ezra.

When I heard the tape, indeed I cried like a baby over the promised good health for Dick, which was one of the best gifts *I* ever got. The music Bilakka composed for us remains the most beautiful I have heard, and I will cherish knowing that when he plays his healing harmonics using *my* hands and *my* fingers, all of this is happening to me and through me.

I have never played an instrument in my life, and couldn't get through chopsticks on the piano, yet Bilakka uses me as a channel to play his "healing music." Dick got weak in the knees the first time he came home and found me "playing." He had come up the back stairs calling, "What record did you buy? It's magnificent." We listen to the tapes of this marvelous music, particularly in times of stress, knowing that music of a higher vibration is absorbed by all of the senses. One of my major frustrations is not being able to "see myself" channeling Bilakka's music. They tell me that the expression on my face is peaceful and my eyes are closed as my fingers race across the keys in glissandos. The delight that the music brings more than compensates for the ache in my fingers and wrists for days thereafter.

Even in our game times with the ETI there are lessons and reminders, but this is a chapter devoted to the fun, and fun it was and is. When I want to unwind, I reach for a deck of cards or a backgammon board. Every night before we go to bed, Dick and I play a game of gin rummy or a game of 'gammon, and we keep a running score. One night when I was losing at gin, I apparently was "out of it" long enough for little Tauri to come through and inform Dick of every card in my hand. She told us the next night, "I do things like that only if they don't matter. I would never do that for you when you were at those tables with the cards and 'bones' "—meaning the casino in Tahoe.

Another time, when we were playing backgammon, Dick commented that Tauri had been there and said that if she were still around it would be nice if she could help him win for a change. He then immediately rolled *four* double sixes in a row to come from way behind to trounce me. Was it Tauri? She declined to say, when asked a few days later. But we knew it couldn't have been anyone else. The odds of rolling out sevens or elevens are one thing, "box cars" are something else!

Getting back to the subject of persiflage—Dick chatted with Cjork about my submitting an article to a monthly magazine which required approximately 2,500 words. Cjork asked, "How many *thoughts* is that?" Sometimes, when Dick or the kids push the ETI for personal information they come back with a lesson instead:

J: Won't you please tell me? Is the answer to my question "no"?
T: I stand on the cosmic amendment, Jill.

J: I guess that means no, doesn't it.

T: Know that silence is not a denial. Delays are not denials. We are all so comfortable with each other now that questions assume a *human* level I do not feel that I can respond to. Do you understand that?

D: She does. I do, too, Tauri.

T: I tell you, the saddest part of the HUMAN humanity is their need for words. In the world of no-language, in the land of thought-reception, in an area large and beautiful-beautiful where concepts are delivered without the use of words, oh, much more is accomplished on a large scale. Many of the lessons we impart are given in silence. Now, little one with hair of bruge, be still. Listen. Think on this. If the truth be known there is no vocabulary at all to make you understand another dimension. *Use the eyes of your mind to replace the ear and listen to the silence. Yes. And learn to respond to those who cry out in silence, for their need is usually more intense than the need of one who bellows for help.*

When I think back to the many lessons we were given on silence, as well as on the use of words, I wonder which ones to share with you. Let me turn the clock back to September 1977. Andrija, Dick, and I were houseguests of a North Carolina gentleman who was thinking of allowing the use of his property for a New Age Community, where selected individuals could come together to work, plan, and study for the era to come. A goodly number of Andrija's Space Kids were there for the better part of a week, so that our host would get to know a nucleus group.

Two of the more articulate and older members—one an engineer and one an author—joined us at the main house early one morning to continue a lively discussion that had started the day before. We were talking about the theory that the speed of light is relative to the number of degrees in a sphere traveled in a given time period, versus another theory that the speed of light is related to a specific linear distance traveled in a given time period.

John, the red-bearded engineer, had been expanding his theory, and Dick had the tape recorder spinning almost the entire time. At one point Tauri had come in, acknowledged Dick and the Space Kids, but ignored our host. After she left, he rather peevishly indicated that he would have loved to talk to her. A few minutes later, when there was a break in the discussion, Dick went to turn a tape over, hesitated, and decided to run the last side of a tape in reverse.

He flipped the switch to "play" and nothing happened. Silence. The same thing happened with his other three reels of tape. After carefully recording the discussion it appeared that his machine had picked up not one word. Suddenly, in came Tauri:

T: Problems, Dick?

D: Ah, Tauri, the machine was going the entire time but now it seems when I go to replay the tapes, there is nothing on them.

T: Amazing! Now let me tell you something. When you think things out—why, that takes quantities of words. More important to finally record the quality of words. Concise thoughts, not ramblings. Wonder of wonders, you now have not taped two hours worth of quantities of words. No.

D: I was worried about the mechanics of the machine because it was running.

T: Is that how your mechanics work?

D: Oh, Tauri, I know this looks pretty crude to you, but it's the only tape recorder I have with me and I'd hate to have it broken.

T: Not broken. Running. Not *recording*, but running and saving your tape and your ears having to listen to all that. Now, first things first. *Hello to you!* [*to our host*] You knew Dick was taping, didn't you, and you wondered why I talked to the one with the beard and not to you before. Well, why would I put a "hello" to the host on a tape that was going to be blank? Now back to work, and let's get it down on tape in ten minutes. Not any longer necessary. And I will come back and let you record what is not on your wondrous machine from the first time I came in, all right? But remember, you with the funny beard, go from ground zero to your conclusion in ten minutes. [TAURI *had corrected* JOHN (*the engineer*) *earlier and returned at precisely the same place to correct him further, once the tape was running and recording.*] He *did* it in ten minutes. Ha-ha! Very good. Now listen to me, all of you. You must go past the reasoning of textbooks. Remember my definition of science: *cosmic revelation*. It is all out there. Discover the principle and you have the invention. *Now* I repeat *hello* to you [*host*], and I say goodbye to *you* [JOHN *and* DICK], and to all of you I say that the tape machine will work perfectly now that you have quality of thoughts instead of quantity of words. [*It worked perfectly.*]

One has to go past the reasoning of textbooks to be able to comprehend what is happening when metal bends. I could write a book on my own metal-bending experiences, but for the persiflage, I turn to one family in my town. The father, a skeptic; the mother, a believer; the three sons, curious. The father changed his mind after he saw how easily I could divide a deck of cards—without looking at them—into reds and blacks. He became even more of a convert after I bent metal for him and his wife, Marilynn, on several occasions in restaurants and in their home.

My funniest experience with our neighbors occurred at home, when the parents and their two older sons came over to look at some of the clippings from the Icelandic newspapers describing my activities at the Frontiers of Physics Conference. The following letter tells the story of the evening's activities:

November 21, 1977

To whom it may concern:

This is to document three separate instances of metal bending by Greta Woodrew of Westport last night.

Mrs. Woodrew's family and my own, dining out at a restaurant in Westport, were waiting for service when Mrs. Woodrew picked up a spoon whose configuration I noted was quite normal, held it lightly between her thumb and forefinger just where the handle reaches the bowl portion, and proceeded to shake the spoon lightly up and down. She did that for about 30 seconds. She then put the spoon back on the table, and it had bent where she had been holding it, perhaps a half inch out of its normal shape—that is, there was a much larger hump, or bend, than the spoon had before.

Mrs. Woodrew then took another spoon, whose configuration I again checked and found to be normal, placed it in a cup, with the handle sticking up at an angle from the cup. Without touching the spoon at all, she ran her hand over it several times, again for perhaps 30 seconds, at which point the spoon handle began to droop down toward the table top. Though she then stopped moving her hand over the spoon, the spoon handle continued to bend and finished with the end of the handle just past the lip of the cup—that is, the handle was just short of being in a U configuration.

Later, at her home, Mrs. Woodrew asked one of my sons for his house key. It was a new key I had recently purchased. She put the key in my older son's hand, in his half-closed fist, and, as best I can describe it, also touched the key and commanded it to bend. My son opened his fist and in fact that same key was both bent and twisted. My son was profoundly affected, realizing that he had retained control of the key, and had inspected it before putting it in his fist. Neither he nor I could find a rational explanation for this phenomenon.

I should record here also an incident which happened last winter. Mrs. Woodrew took a deck of my cards, brand new, and after I myself had shuffled the cards thoroughly, held the cards face down in her hand and proceeded to deal them off into two piles. One pile she said would have all the red cards, the other all the blacks. She went through all 52 cards, one by one, then turned each pile over and in fact had correctly identified which were black and which were red. She had not missed one. Her husband indicated that Mrs. Woodrew had accomplished the same feat three times before, and had missed only a single card on a fourth occasion. My wife and I tried independently then and thereafter, many times, and could come up at best with 50-50 or 40-60.

I should note that I come to this area of activity with rather advanced skepticism. All of these experiences suggest to me that complete skepticism is no longer tenable.

This documentation in no way indicates an official IBM observation or conclusion. It is my own.

> Howard M. Greenwald
> Director of Communications
> Data Processing Division

So few people are willing to put these things down on paper that I am delighted to be able to thank Howard publicly for his cooperation and immediate response at that time.

But Howard's letter does not tell what happened the following day when the Greenwalds' youngest son—a handsome twelve-year-old whom I fondly refer to as The Cookie Monster—arrived on my doorstep demanding that I bend metal for him.

"Not now," I said. His mother and I were having coffee together at the time and my mind was on other matters.

"Aw, gee, c'mon and bend it, *if* you really *can*," he insisted.

"I won't even try now, Cookie Monster," I told him firmly.

His mother and I finished our coffee, and as they were both leaving, the youngster turned to her, and in great disgust announced, "I *knew* she really couldn't do it anyway!"

The rest of the Cookie Monster's family do not agree. Number Two son is still trying to get back his key that bent in the hands of his brother, but Number One son carries it around and shows no signs of ever parting with it. In addition, the oldest boy wrote an A paper on extrasensory perception for his high school class, and I am told that he and his classmates have some fascinating discussions about all sorts of cosmic possibilities.

I'm not surprised. This is a Star Trek generation, and the young people of today don't have as much to relearn as our generation does. They "dig it."

T: They *dig* it?
D: They understand it.
T: Oh. Yes. I dig it!

16

What's the "Matter"?

A YOUNG MAN named Michael has been a student of mine for well over a decade. I introduced him to yoga, to Reflex Balance, and to rooting: the concept of energy being drawn up from the living ball of matter we call Earth. I taught Michael to see auras, and after that he began to withdraw from the physical world of karate (he is a Fifth-degree Black Belt in Tai Chi Chuan-Kempo) and to move toward a synthesis of mental and physical activity. In teaching this exceptional student, I myself developed surges of energy I never knew existed.

One day an entity named Master Ching, a Karate Grand Master, used me as a channel. Visualize the first time we met this unlikely character ("we" being Michael, Dick, and a couple of my children who were home for the day). Master Ching came through the channel, assumed a very low "fight stance" with his knees almost touching the ground, and began to circle around Michael. He demonstrated pressure point techniques and survival katas which Michael said were so incredibly fast, advanced, and graceful that there was no contest in the "fighting" that they did. According to Michael, he hadn't a chance against Master Ching. *I* haven't a chance against Ching either! My body is one royal mess after he takes over my vehicle. I've learned to live with muscle cramps and charleyhorses, which I put up with cheerfully because of the wondrous things Ching teaches Michael in an art of which I know absolutely nothing.

The Grand Master allowed himself to be photographed using the channel and later, when I saw the look on Michael's face—wary, alert—and the Oriental look in my own eyes, I knew my aches and pains were worthwhile.

One day Master Ching gave Michael a lesson on the breaking of boards and rocks with the open hand. After I was back in control of my vehicle, Mike told me about the lesson. Ching had suggested that they try to get in tune with the rock, then go out and split one in this barehanded method. When I say "suggested," I mean that Ching indicated his desire through gesture. Ching does not speak while in the channel, but it is never necessary. He usually makes his intent quite clear, but if by any chance we misinterpret his gestures, Tauri invariably comes through to rectify the confusion—just as she came through after our first meeting with Ching, to tell us his name and a bit of his history.

Mike and I went outside and selected a huge rock which we could barely lift. After some deep breathing, he slowly lifted his hand, I counted one, two, three, and he let his hand drop to the rock in the soft-break technique. The rock remained intact but Mike's hand began to swell. He tried it again and the same thing happened. Then suddenly, I was inspired to suggest that I stand behind Mike and summon up the Earth's energy. I would then put my hand lightly on top of his, and we would drop our hands together on the rock. Mike and I did some preparatory deep breathing, and after the one, two, three count, dropped our hands, mine over his, onto the rock. Although we touched it with very little force, the rock split wide open and fell into two pieces. We were so stunned and thrilled that we decided to try the same technique on another boulder. Twice we tried, and twice we failed.

Then came a familiar voice:

T: Once should be enough for anybody!

M: Oh, Tauri, I should have known you were helping us!

T: Helping, yes. Doing, no. Of course, I may have leaned on *her* hand a little! You and my channel got in tune with the rock. Do you understand what you did? What my channel did? Develop the ability to bring your consciousness to the vibratory level of the rock at will.

I know that singers with the ability to duplicate the vibration of a piece of crystal can amplify the vibration until the resonance, the level of energy, becomes so great that it shatters the glass. Were we working on the same principle? We do know that in resonance, energy can be transferred. Did the splitting of the rock resemble the shattering of crystal stemware? Or did we turn up the volume on the rock's radio band to such a high level that we shattered the receiver?

When I was in school, all the physics we learned was built upon the principles advanced by Sir Isaac Newton. Newton's laws were based upon the scientist's observation of the everyday world; they put things into a mechanical model that predicted events in the macroscopic world that were subsequently proven. The world that we know, and the universe that we suspected—but could not observe—were understandable because physics dealt with things that our senses could perceive, even if they needed some mechanical help. Newton structured the universe in logical, rational, mechanical, and comprehensible terms for the human mind.

Toward the end of the nineteenth century, physicists developed the experiments that proved the existence of the atom. The unlocking of that mystery led to many interesting experiments and subsequently provided answers to the riddles of the Universe. It also led to a world of physics beyond Sir Isaac Newton, a world in which the laws of Newton do not apply. It revealed to us that the great laws of physics are indeed subject to revision, ever-constant scrutiny, and paradigm change. Physics is by no means a conclusive discipline, nor should we conceive of it as such. Established scientific bases are continually being discredited and being replaced by new and more encompassing theories. At our present stage of development we cannot look to three-dimensional scientific experiments to offer the final solutions for ultimate explanations.

And so, it was discovered that the atom pulses, vibrates, sends out its message at a frequency of 10^{15}. This figure in round numbers comes to 10,000,000,000,000,000. The atom pulses that many times every second! If our senses had the apparatus to receive this frequency and convert it to the electrical impulses that our brain interprets, we could tune into—communicate—with an atom. We can't, and neither can the technology we have developed so far.

As these atoms interact with other atoms and form the molecules that we know as the elements of our material world, the rate of pulsing slows down. These elements, all ninety-two of them, pulse at their own frequencies, and so send out their individual songs. Our technology has instrumentation to pick up and identify these frequencies. Science knows the number of times each of the elements pulses per second and can identify the element by this pulsing. These are the voices of the elements—the frequency upon which they communicate. Those on the "inside," using the buzz words of physics, say that these are the "discrete frequencies" of the elements.

As these elements combine with themselves and with other elements, they build up complex molecules whose voices are less shrill. They pulse much more slowly and communicate in a language that we can understand because our senses—which are a network of responses to pulsations—can receive them. R. Buckminster Fuller says,

Things make themselves known through PATTERNS OF RECURRENCE . . . patterned solicitations of our 5 senses. They interact so reliably that we speak of inhabiting a world of things. Stable pulsings of molecules against the molecules in a fingertip is registered through electrified nerve ends as a solid table.

These molecules organize themselves into systems of organic and inorganic matter—the matter which makes up our perceived reality.

With this kind of background information to enlighten us, we were approaching an understanding of how Michael and I had split that huge rock. If everything that we know as matter pulses, then it was logical that our five senses, our radio bands, were tuned in to only a portion of this pulsing. Mike and I had extended our radio bands to "get in tune with the rock." Once in tune we had amplified the frequency of the rock, increased its level of energy beyond its abilities to retain its shape, and like the crystal glass, it shattered. As Benjamin Franklin wrote, "It is impossible to imagine the height to which may be carried—the power of man over matter."

Our feat was mind-boggling, yes; but impossible, no. It indicated that humans *had* this ability to tune into far more vibrations than our senses "mislead" us to believe. The great Indian philosopher, Patanjali, in his Yoga Aphorisms, seemed to agree: "The materialists—those who describe themselves as being 'down to earth'—are the ones who are living in an unreal world, because they limit themselves to the level of gross sense-perception."

Once I had discovered the pulsing activity of matter, a question began to form in my mind. Dick and I had witnessed dematerialization on a number of occasions. We had watched each episode in amazement, but written them all off to ETI activity beyond the comprehension and ability of man. Now we asked ourselves this question: if we were to change the pulsing of these systems to a frequency beyond the ability of our senses to tune in, would we be causing a dematerialization?

We immediately wondered if this might be the explanation for another remarkable occasion when the form of a piece of matter was altered. Dick and I were having a late steak dinner at the Brown Derby restaurant after a hectic business day in Tallahassee, Florida. Shortly after we were served, Tauri came in to look in amazement at our—as she put it—"eating the cow." Five college students were cutting up noisily at a nearby table, and Tauri asked Dick if they were disturbing him and giving him "head noises." She went on to say that if their chatter was bothersome, she would "blow up their bottles of beer onto their laps."

Dick assured her once more that he had no "head noises," and Tauri left the channel as abruptly as she had come. She returned at dessert time, however. Always one to use what she refers to as "our lingo" (and making increasing use of our idioms in her own vocabulary), she announced, "I bopped back in."

Dick kiddingly asked, "Did you come to see the expression on *my* face if you were to shatter *my* glass?"

"*No!*" Tauri shot back, "*hers!*"

With that my parfait glass split into two even shiny unsplintered pieces—Tauri was gone—and I was back and staring at my parfait lying in two chunks on the tablecloth. The waiter who was serving our coffee stared, too, and in the process, poured coffee all over the table. Dick and I managed to look nonchalant—although to this day, I don't know how.

Extraterrestrials apparently have no problem extending their radio bands to get in tune with whatever objects they wish. We have seen them do this on numerous other occasions. One night they rearranged our living room so that objets d'art were placed in the most ludicrous places. One minute we would be looking at our twenty-four-pound marble falcon on a table, and the next minute it would be on a high shelf across the way. A ceramic eagle invisibly flew from one end of the room and took up its perch at the other. Our marble statue of Pierrot, that weighs hundreds of pounds, changed position from the center of the fireplace ledge to the picture window on the right. We were in the room throughout this entire, incredible performance, and although we could only tune in to the results, it left us breathless. *Technology!* That's what Tauri told us it was, a more advanced technology. As soon as we on Earth receive the "cosmic revelation" that unlocks this technology, we too will be able to materialize and dematerialize objects in this way.

Tauri recently gave us an analogy to describe the level at which our current state of technology stands in relation to the levels we can some day attain:

T: When early man became aware of the tree, he was in his most primitive state. He learned that the tree could be used to protect him from the direct rays of the Sun . . . give him shade. A little later on he discovered that the fruit on the tree was good to eat. Progress was made when man discovered he could strip the bark of the tree, or hollow the trunk of the tree, and make an object that could carry him on top of the water. Next man took that bark of the tree, stretched it, and used it to write on to make records and pictures of things that happened . . . and so on and on and on. . . . *In your technology you are still only eating the fruit.*

One problem with which I constantly wrestle is my lack of waking memory when I return from being "out there" receiving instructions. ETI assure me that when the time is right the lessons will "be there" because memory is a "secondary thought-wave." I do, however, have vivid memories of the colors and music I see and hear "out there." There are no words to describe these wondrous things, because one sees and *hears* the colors on heightened sensory bands. One hears and *sees* the music.

I began to realize that music was the identifying mark of the Ogatta group—a certain group of frequencies played as their anthem of uniqueness in the Cosmos—their theme of "discrete frequencies." Music identifies all other civilizations as well. I always felt free to "follow the music" to "get out there." When strains of exquisite intensity flood my head, I know that I am about to get out of my body and I relax willingly. I was cautioned from the very beginning to "Be sure to know your music . . . *our* music." That message was and still is repeated regularly.

It was in July 1977 that we learned the true importance of distinguishing the music or the frequencies that play in the Cosmos. Dick and I were in our bedroom chatting with our son Alan about the work we had begun to do. Suddenly I thought I heard the music of the Ogatta group, and I let myself be lured "out there." I followed the music up the pathway I had been taught to use. It was the wrong music and the wrong road. In following this wrong music, my vehicle was left vulnerable, open and unguarded. It was not the music of the Ogatta group. It belonged to those whom our ETI had lightly dubbed "the kookies"—those entities who were not positive, sympathetic beings, and who are quite capable of taking over a vehicle and using it for their own ends.

What followed was another case of matter being easily altered. As Dick tells the story, a strange look crossed my face and was then quickly replaced by an unfamiliar expression. I appeared to hold my breath and puff out my cheeks. At first, Alan and Dick thought I was clowning around to relieve the tensions of the rather serious conversation in which we had been engaged. Moments later, they realized that some strange entity was in the channel and that the channel was holding her breath and turning bright red, her eyes bulging. In horror, they watched the scene which they recorded as follows:

She stood there, rooted to the ground, and turned a bright red, almost blue, and her eyes glittered although they appeared narrow. She appeared to get taller, but in a moment we heard a "pop" and we saw that she was not getting taller, but getting larger. Fatter. She was swelling up like a balloon. The pop we heard turned out to be the button flying off the waistline of her skirt which fell to the floor. Her diaphragm seemed to be extended and her waistline swollen. A rasping sound proved to be her brassiere hooks pulling apart and twisting angularly in the back. She stood there and we couldn't budge her and she held her breath and stayed red and awful for what seemed an eternity to us. In reality, it lasted about fifteen minutes. No matter how we shook her we couldn't budge her or stop that breath holding. Once she was back with us she seemed completely bewildered. Her skirt was on the floor and her bra was hanging down. Her arms and legs looked slender as always, but her midsection, back, and stomach were puffed out. She looked down at herself and whispered, "Oh, my God" over and over. She ignored us and walked into the bathroom and stepped onto the scale and said in a very confused voice, "Alan . . . Dick . . . how come I gained eighteen pounds?" (Within the next forty-eight hours it was to be thirty pounds.)

When I was "with it" again, Dick and Alan instinctively tried to soothe me. They reassured me that it was nothing, that it would be gone in the morning, etc. They used every cliché and platitude in the book, and because I wanted to believe them and was both confused and uncommonly tired, I heeded their advice and went to bed. Dick and Alan stayed by my side, watching and waiting until Tauri came through much later that night. She was not her usual happy self.

T: It took those kookies a tremendous amount of energy to bring upon a subject so much force. My channel drifted because she mistook their music for our own. How clever of them, how frightening for her. She must learn to differentiate with clarity and never be tricked.

A: Who are they, Tauri? Why would they do such a thing to Mom?

T: Who "they" are doesn't matter, Alan. Another name from the Cosmos. I tell you that what does matter is that the work she is to do is vital to your planet in the future and they would like to see her step away from her commitment. I will tell you that these things usually escalate for a couple of your days. She will probably have double the weight put onto her. Pumped on, you might say.

D: Thirty-six pounds??

T: Maybe. Maybe. But, there are laws out here and they cannot do anything of this sort again for a long, long time. No, they will not be heard from again for a very long period, if ever. It's as if you have just so many of your coins to spend and you can dole them out or you can just . . . what is your lingo . . . "blow it" on one big thing. They blew it all on this one thing.

D: What will happen to her body with all that weight "pumped on," as you say?

T: She will have to live with it for some time.

D: You mean it won't disappear the way it came? She'll stay blown up?

T: Dick, they literally attacked her. As long as they do *not* come back and as long as she understands *why* they want her out of the picture, I would not fret too much. Yes, the weight will be a troublesome sight and feeling for her. She wants to look trim and attractive and you both want for her to look and feel pretty. But we are now dealing in energies and they work in strange ways to your thinking. Your technology has not accounted for this kind of thing yet.

D: How will we know when this "energy" has stopped working on her?

T: I have to go out there. [*pause*] You asked how long before the energy stops working. Know that although this is an artificial weight, it is also a *physical reality*. It will be at least two moons, maybe three. But you will know when that one big shot has stopped, and when it has, she will have to be careful about what she eats and she can take it off very slowly but very surely.

A: By two or three moons you mean months, Tauri? Mom will stay this way for that long? She'll have fits!

T: My dear Alan, you with the holes in your face, you will tell her that she can and will take it off, but that the important thing is not to be discouraged or they are winners and she, and we, are losers. We will explain it to her.

The next two days were a horror story for me. The one thing we have always stressed in our family is physical fitness. We are all athletes who love to ski, swim, and play tennis. Now here I was like an uncoordinated blimp with thin arms and legs attached to a body that not only looked grotesque but ached all over.

I wouldn't go out, I was depressed. And on top of all this, I literally had nothing to wear. In those forty-eight hours, I had expanded from a size ten to a size sixteen!

I was determined to get rid of my excess weight before the two or three months Tauri spoke of, so I fasted for two days. My scale didn't move an ounce. Testing, I ate a cream cheese and jelly sandwich and had a malted milk. I weighed in again, and again my weight didn't vary by so much as an ounce. Whether I starved or gorged myself, it appeared that I was going to look bloated and weird for at least two months before I could even hope to reduce. "Why me?" I agonized. *"What do I need this for?"*

It was October first before my horrendous experience finally came to an end, and I was able to start losing weight. The excess pounds didn't melt or drop away at the rate they had appeared; they came off in a disgustingly slow normal fashion—which, as every dieter knows, is much too slow.

It took a full eight months, but eventually, through a regimen of exercising, yoga, and dieting, all thirty-plus pounds disappeared. I have never felt quite the same since then. As a matter of fact, while I reduced to a size twelve, my dimensions were not the same. I felt—and am—"thicker."

During my first two months of being overweight, I was gently teased by my daughters for looking like a hippie. This was because I refused to invest in a wardrobe of size sixteens and instead took to wearing loose-fitting sacks and muumuus. Because any clothing that bound was uncomfortable, I also stopped wearing a bra. (I, who had constantly chastised both my daughters whenever I caught them trying to leave the house braless!)

The humorous side of my sudden weight gain was that people who had seen me only days before didn't know what to say when they saw me now! The exterminator, the Fuller Brush man, our housekeeper, business candidates, clients, all the friends who came and went without having any idea of the work I was involved in. My ETI life was a "closet" experience, so I could hardly explain what had happened. My mother, who tends to overweight, constantly rebuked me for letting myself go. When I finally resumed my almost normal size, she exclaimed, "It's about time you decided to take pride in the way you look!"

Unfortunately, I was victimized a second time with another twenty-five-pound addition to my by-then slender frame. It happened more than two years later and I am still in the throes of laboriously taking off that all too visible—if artificially produced—weight that carried me right back to a size sixteen. The episode took place in front of my poor husband who was frightened and utterly powerless to help me as he watched me blow up. This time the weight gain was instantaneous without any forty-eight-hour lag, and incredibly did not show immediately on my scale. On any scale. It was not too difficult, however, to guesstimate the twenty-five-pound weight gain based on my dimensions and clothing. An "energy pump-up" played havoc with my body—and spirits. A week or two after the fact, the actual poundage registered on the scales as well as on my frame.

Some hours after the second bombardment, my Destiny Screen rolled and provided the following answers to our many questions about this weird and horrifying phenomenon:

1. As they expend, she expands. The difference of one letter is significant.
2. Think in terms of our technology of *gases* . . . not energy. Think helium and its conversion.

3. Never lose sight of the fact that everything ties back to a law and order in the Universe, not only behavioral patterns.
4. We must go back to the same Second Law of Thermodynamics. Unfinished formula of Einstein. Extension of the formula of Newton.

We still do not completely understand these answers but we did understand, quite clearly, that the Ogatta group was incensed. I was given instruction with memory on recognizing their music and learning to distinguish it from any other. I was also told to "ride my slide of light" as taught—seeing my music and hearing my color blue—and I pray that I will not be victimized again.

I feel that the kookies expended their last large dosage of energy that will ever again hit me. No more will my body be the kind of pulsing matter that can be altered from one physical form to another in the twinkling of an eye. I know my music, the music of the Ogatta group. As for the others out there, they play a very different tune.

17

The Scenario

WHEN I learned to type, I memorized the sentence, "Now is the time for all good men to come to the aid of their country." As I come to this section and struggle to commit to paper what I know I must, that sentence suddenly comes back to me with far more force than it had during my typing exercises. It haunts me as I set down chapter and verse of this story which belongs to every being on this planet. Tauri's dictum to "keep it light" abandons me. The hard facts cannot be softened. It is a Scenario of destruction and construction, failure and hope, darkness and promise.

In recounting my experiences, words have often failed me—in most cases because there was no appropriate vocabulary for the phenomena I wished to describe or explain. But for the Scenario that has been given to us, the words are all too clear; they are words that we all know which describe Nature's activities in stark strokes.

"Tell them," I have been prodded again and again. "You must tell them. Humankind must prepare for what is to come. Trumpet the voice and scribe the pen." Tell them, not only to entertain them with badinage, not just to broaden their horizons and perhaps "bobble their minds," but to open their eyes; shake them up, warn them. Tell them so that they will know and you can allay their fears. "But tell them first of free will." Tell them that predictions are dangerous unless one realizes that free will, human behavior, action, reaction can alter *any* prediction.

T: Do you know, that if your human beings "as one" were to change what you call their "consciousness" all at once, *none* of your Scenario . . . and ours . . . would come to pass. But you know and I know that all humanity will not change "consciousness" simultaneously, in a golden moment, *on a slide of light*. More is the pity. So, the Scenario stands. It is a prediction based on behavior patterns as they exist now.

Part of your mission is to tell the people what is to come so that they may be prepared and not afraid. After you start to trumpet the voice, you must scribe the pen and tell them.

"Tell them." This was the only *directive* I received from our ETI friends because the rest, as you know, was *direction*. I think back to the day they first rolled my Destiny Screen. It defied linear time. It defied natural law as we currently define it. Imagine seeing future events rolled before my eyes! No, I don't have to search for words when I describe what my Destiny Screen revealed. It is the same vision of destruction that I described at the beginning of this book.

Hurricanes. Floods. Super magnetic storms. Droughts. Earthquakes. Volcanoes. Tidal waves that buried whole cities and their populations beneath a wall of water. People dying of thirst and hunger. People with burns on their bodies. Animals with hair scorched and eyes glazed. Extinction of much wildlife, furbearers, species of birds. I witnesssed with horror the devastation of our beautiful planet.

But as my Destiny Screen rolled, I was told that I was looking at the survivors of what is to come. And then the message came clear: *"Despite what man can do to man, and Nature's plan, there are those civilizations out there in the Cosmos who believe that Planet Earth is worth helping in its time of great adjustments."*

I witnessed the devastation of our planet, and it was not in the dim and distant future. It was in my own lifetime. In the coming decades. It had started already. And I wept for humanity. Then I began to view the Scenario in its entirety. I started to understand the signs for what they were, and soon I could face it more calmly, with a love and faith in our ETI friends. These marvelous beings, with their advanced technologies, minds, and spirits, had promised their aid. They were going to share their universal knowledge with us on Spaceship Planet Earth. They gave promise to help guide us into the New Age.

After my Destiny Screen rolled, I went back to the transcript of the tape of August 31, 1977, when we had participated in the Mind Link. I was the channel and Tauri spoke:

T: I would like to talk to you about things past and about things in the future. You are not gathered here lightly. *Architects of the future,* we call you! You *are* "architects," you know. Architects for what is to come. Let us not glimpse it with fear, but with a calm knowledge that you will help other survivors accept what Nature's dictates will be. Fire. Famine. Floods. Nature's holocaustic endeavors to cleanse Planet Earth in the way she knows best. We talk about architects— the young who will build the new buildings, harnessing Sun's energy. As Sun wreaks its own holocaust, so it sends back its beams to heal. Same to be said for Moon: tidal waves, hurricanes. *Moon.* Moon light. *Light*, as from the Sun, *not* heat, but light. *That* is a key you must unlock here! Yes, "architects" you will be, growing foods that do not need refrigeration, healthy things to nourish human frames. *Healers* you must be, healers as masses of people come to you for what they think of as miracles! And they are *not* miracles. But as skin closes over and so-called "media" records it, "Oh!" they will say out there, "A miracle!" And *we* say, "Oh, no, not a miracle but a latching-on to energy which makes these things not miracles, but *cosmic revelations*." Our definition of science and of miracles: cosmic revelations. Some things have been revealed to you in your days together. Do you know how much there is to be unlocked by the architects of the future just from a springboard of what you have actually witnessed here? Vibrations! Harmonics! Things to grow and use in many ways in and on your bodies. Twenty-four-plus civilizations wait and look, and say to you to ride that slide of light that you may see for yourselves what was revealed to my channel. Others may join you in a similar attempt at this very hour, and they too sit and listen in other tongues. Do it! Be as one. Be very still.

and later . . .

When you are strong enough to climb such a mountain, you must be strong enough to come back down. What do you find at the bottom of that mountain but step one of the ladder to the next mountain you must climb. This is your mission. This is your job. You have agreed to do it. Lovely though it is, you must come back. Architects, you young ones, building for your planet. Teachers and communicators, you elders, finding more young ones and merging them in. Yes!

and later . . .

Remember the coming of the gattae. All those on Vesta are working to make the loops for the gattae to come—and come they will, with you or without you, come they will. Direct communications will be directed to some in this group who will be present at the landings. These crafts will be seen first in small groups and then in larger ones and then by huge masses of people. And those of you who are properly trained will be the ones to say to your people, "Here! Here! They are *benign!*" You will each know the craft or gattae from your own civilization, whichever it may be. Know your "music." Know the sounds of your home civilization. Know that we want to help Planet Earth in its time of great transition.

There was more. I think back to the lessons on telepathizing.

Be still! Develop the ability to clear the mind. The easiest thing in the world to do is send a message out but it's a bit harder to receive it and understand it. Find the right ones to practice with. Someone with whom you are "in tune." Tell them to play the game simply: send just a color. A number. A shape. Something simple. Send it out, and when it is received, have it sent back to you. Soon you will find it quite easy. You see, when man plays his tricks on man, and Nature has her way, communications will break down. Communication systems such as you are accustomed to. Wires will fall to the ground, useless. Telephones will not function. The television sets will just be boxes without pictures. Do you see what people will need? *Mind control for messages to be sent over what you think of as "distance."* Control the mind's energy. It is necessary, not wondrous, to be able to send and receive a message through the energy, controlled, by the mind. *Eventually you will not need words, just thoughts. Such is our telepathy.*

As I reflect on the Mind Link experience, when I first saw bits and pieces of the Scenario rolled before my eyes, I realize how much that experience confirmed the Scenario, if not the time sequence, that had been described to my family at that memorable Thanksgiving dinner back in 1976. I also think back to a brief dialogue between Dick and Tauri that was recorded almost a year later.

T: Make the most of every day, every blink, every moon, because time as you know it is short when you consider the type of life you are leading now. Human beings must be strong. They must be prepared. My channel and others must get out the words and the concepts with all the strength in their hearts and hands and heads.

D: When you say the time is short, can you give us some number in terms of years?

T: Let us just say, dear Ezra, that you all will be looking at a different face to your planet, a different world in the decades now begun before the turn of your century. In but a few blinks of time, minds must come together. Those who cannot take it, those who do not wish to take it, those who are too weak to take it, and those who will not train to take it will burn out.

D: You speak of those who are training now?

T: Yes, and more. There will be others. I again say to you that with you or without you those things will happen. We of the Ogatta group want it to happen with your help, your energy, your understanding. One mind, one energy. The very look of Earth will shift. This is the reason we stress the necessity to learn to grow things which do not need refrigeration—electricity. Mental radio must be developed and is vital to survival for when media is cut off, each will be the means of communication. *Everthying we have told you ties together.* No information is given lightly although we keep it light in its presentation. So must my channel "keep it light" when she addresses the people.

D: You told us that we must not take the time "one on one" to teach the many who approach us daily. How in the world can we prepare?

T: You sadden me, dear Dick. There is a law and an order in the Universe. I can tell you *to* prepare but I cannot always tell you *how*. Remember free will. My channel's mission is to tell the story of the coming of the gattae. *Her mission is to alert the people and allay their ungrounded fears.* She will do it on her feet, with you at her side, and she will do it with the pen, with you next to her. Together, between your thinking, word must go out that those who are on the gattae will bring with them new and advanced technologies for Planet Earth. Take it all one step at a time.

Taking it one step at a time has not been an easy task, but this much I know: time and space have little meaning when you travel in the Cosmos. There is infinite space but precious little time as we know it. The seeds of the mind must be sown *NOW* so that the fruits can be shared by all humankind. Every act causes a chain of events. Think a random thought, and its vibrations will continue endlessly out into the Cosmos, bumping and interacting with other waves, creating an interference pattern. Throw a stone into a pool, and waves will be set in motion which do not stop even when the stone reaches the bottom. I now throw my stone and, in so doing, hope to set in motion waves of thought. I throw the stone of the

Scenario into the pool of human consciousness with a confidence that those who read the signs—and interpret them—will not be afraid as these changes and transitions begin to occur.

In the not too distant future, I hope to be one of the communicators between the gattae, or spacecraft, which you, and others who witness the landings, may be calling UFOs. The Ogatta group has invested a great deal of time and energy in my training so that I could forewarn you of this Scenario that *will* come to pass in our lifetime—that is, in fact, already happening—and allay the fears of those who do not understand. In linking communications with these advanced civilizations, humans will progress up the evolutionary ladder. We on Planet Earth will be the beneficiaries of new technologies, new means of communications, and new ways of handling our new existence.

Twenty-four civilizations with far greater technology than we currently possess are committed to helping Planet Earth make its torturous transition. After many changes there will follow a brighter tomorrow—albeit a different sort of tomorrow—for future generations of human beings.

Question: How can I best serve these entities in helping us when most governments are dedicated to suppressing the knowledge of their very existence? Answer: I can best serve by preparing *you* for their arrival, for come they will. They are coming here to help. They are *benign*. They bring advanced techniques and knowledge to help move us into the next stage. They will be seen first by small groups, and then by larger groups. When they arrive, remember the purpose of their visit: to give aid to us in our time of need. You need not have *fear*. Do not *panic*. Tell this to those around you. Fear of the unknown is one of humankind's greatest enemies. It keeps us from acting rationally, sanely. Panics are the result of surprise! We will need all our wits about us to help us survive "Nature's plan . . . and what man can do to man." We will need the technology which the ETIs offer to share. If good fortune smiles upon you, *you* will be in one of the groups that is privileged to meet them. I wish it for your sake.

18

UFOs and IFOs

SOME OF the activity "out there" has already begun to manifest "down here." Humans have given it a label that reflects the breadth of their understanding: Unidentified Flying Objects. UFOs are a phenomenon that many Americans see, many discuss, and a clear majority, according to a 1978 Gallup poll, believe in.

When a mystifying object appears in our sky, we try to find a logical explanation. It could be any number of things—a comet, swamp gas, lunar halo, weather balloon, satellite, shooting star, ball lightning, sun flare, planet, holographic image, or the Northern lights. If none of these logical labels fit, we try some illogical ones: a hoax, flying saucer, hallucination (individual or mass), psychic projection, heavenly angel, or mirage. Most of the time, however, one of the logical labels works and the UFO becomes an IFO, an Identified Flying Object. But what about those other objects that defy labeling?

During the past thirty-two years, *over* one hundred sightings of UFOs have been reported nightly around the world. According to a series aired on WNEW-TV News in New York, in February 1978, 2,000 of the more than 36,500 sightings each year are by Americans. The figure is even more impressive when you consider that fewer people venture out at night, and that according to one reliable estimate, only 13 percent of the people who do spot something "unidentifiable" in the air report it, for fear of ridicule or adverse publicity.

I have read many reports about UFOs. They all vary in their estimations of how many of these objects actually are identifiable. Some experts claim 75 percent; others put the figure as high as 98 percent. But what of the remaining 25 percent—or even 2 percent, for that matter. Two percent of 36,500 is 730; 730 sightings per year times 30 years is 21,900. That's hardly a figure that can be ignored.

In March 1978, a Gallup poll projected that some 13 million Americans had seen UFOs. That's one out of nine people in the USA. The McDonnell-Douglas Corporation, a prime contractor for NASA, currently has more than 92,000 cases of sightings in its computer banks. Big numbers, these. Moreover, there has been a high degree of confirmation in quite a number of the cases.

Interestingly, when 2,199 UFO reports were analyzed by specialists under contract to the Air Force, the conclusion was that 33 percent had to be classified as "unidentifiable." Not 2 percent or 25 percent, but *33 percent*—726 of them. Nevertheless, Project Blue Book, the final phase of a twenty-year study by the Air Force, was used to publicly discredit the existence of the UFOs. According to J. Allen Hynek, who spoke freely before the WNEW-TV cameras, the Air Force went into the study believing UFOs were nonexistent. Dr. Hynek, former head and Professor Emeritus of the Astronomy Department at Northwestern University, served as the chief *debunker* for the Air Force during the early part of his twenty years with them. He has since reversed his position, convinced that the subject is worthy of scientific study. He now criticizes the Air Force for its rigid "it can't be, therefore it isn't" type of thinking.

On July 31, 1980, WINS news radio station quoted Dr. Hynek as saying that on June 14, sightings were made in forty cities in five South American countries. The reports came from "highly responsible people." He remarked that two mysteries were involved: "One, the UFOs themselves, and two, how the subject was treated."

Dick and I flew to Chicago to meet with Dr. Hynek on August 15. "The study of UFOs should be accorded respect although it's seemingly weird—seemingly strange," he told us. "The subject has never been treated professionally. It should be approached in the same way we would any scientific discipline. The UFO refuses to go away. It is a phenomenon of our times."

Since most people do not report UFO sightings or encounters for fear of ridicule or because they do not know where to go to get a fair hearing, they join what Dr. Hynek called "the legion of the bewildered silent." They can, he assured me, always contact the Center for UFO Studies, P.O. Box 1402, Evanston, Illinois. He serves as its scientific director.

A great deal of the information I have garnered about UFOs has come from people who wish to remain anonymous for fear of ridicule or losing their credibility or even their jobs. This is especially true of airline pilots who will only talk "off the record." I therefore learned with great interest that Swiss Air reports its sightings regularly to the Center for UFO Studies. Bravo, Swiss Air!

WNEW's excellent, week-long television series raised some other interesting points. "The government takes the position that 95 percent of all reports are hogwash," one newscaster noted.

This from a President who publicly claimed to have seen a UFO and originally campaigned to do something about it? A man who said he would "get to the bottom of this phenomenon"?

And then there's the Air Force official who told the television reporter, "If a government agent doesn't take the pictures, there is reason to believe that the film is suspect." Isn't that a bit narrow? Well, no more narrow than NASA, which keeps disclaiming any known contact with the UFOs, directly contradicting the statements made by its own former private consultant, Dr. James Hurtak. Hurtak, who is now the director of the Academy for Future Science, has concrete evidence of UFO contact, based on taped sounds emanating from a spacecraft.

I don't know who NASA thinks it's fooling when it issues public statements declaring that "nothing has been kept secret from the American public." Astronaut Gordon Cooper tells of a day at Edwards Air Force Base in California when several film crews were present and a UFO was sighted in a dry lake bed. The crews filmed it and turned the film over to NASA for safekeeping. It was never seen again. During his space mission in March 1969, astronaut James McDivitt took seventy-two frames of 16-millimeter footage of a UFO. NASA called the resultant pictures "sun flares; sun reflections off the wing." The day that McDivitt took his shots, there was some urine spillage in his rocket cabin. NASA further discounted the photos by claiming that, due to the spillage, McDivitt may have had an "eye irritation." I can't help wondering if the NASA spokesman thought the camera had bladder and ocular problems as well.

Former Apollo astronaut Edgar Mitchell compiled a comprehensive review of psychic research in his book, *Psychic Explorations*. "A psychic event is a reality, and psychic exploration is a challenge for *science* that can no longer be denied, avoided, ignored," he wrote. Close friends of Mitchell say that while he was on his space mission in February 1971, he saw something that propelled him into psychic research.

Gordon Cooper and five other Apollo astronauts are said to have seen UFOs, followed UFOs, or been followed by UFOs. John Glenn believes in them. World War I ace Eddie Rickenbacker stated unequivocally: "Flying saucers are real. Too many good men have seen them who do not 'hallucinate.' "

Whatever your political preferences, you must keep an open mind when our elected officials speak out on such matters. They tend to be reluctant to risk the ridicule of a constituency that holds the keys to their next paycheck. And yet, former Ohio Governor John Gilligan doesn't mind admitting, "I saw one." Richard Nixon was planning to release the information gathered by government agencies on UFOs on Labor Day, 1974, but other matters intervened. Senator Barry Goldwater is a believer. And, of course, Jimmy Carter.

Back in 1969, when Mr. Carter was governor of the state of Georgia, he spotted a UFO in the town of Leary, Georgia. Mr. Carter, a graduate in nuclear physics, filed an official report with NICAP— the National Investigations Committee of Aerial Phenomena—on the sighting. Ten other men were with him at the time. The craft hovered within about 300 yards of the group. Later, Carter made the public statement: "If I become president, I'll make every piece of information that this country has about UFO sightings available to the public. I am convinced that UFOs exist, because I have seen one."

Well, the erstwhile governor became president of the United States, but officials in his administration were quoted as saying that any investigation of UFOs would be "a futile undertaking." Still another public statement on the matter was that the Carter administration regards anything to do with UFO studies as "will-o'-the-wisp." I suggest you check your dictionary definition of that expression. I think you'll find it an eye-opener.

It is obvious that both NASA and the United States government are suppressing information on UFOs. This cosmic Watergate is not very convincing. A consensus of UFO sighters believe that the American government is unwilling, rather than unable, to give definitive answers to an intrigued public. UFO believers are *non*-believers in a government that repeatedly stonewalls on relevant information—especially since there are so many well-equipped monitoring stations all over this country. Many of us wonder just what is being concealed, and why. One Washington source told me cryptically, "UFO secrecy is due in large part to a twenty-eight-year-old decision made by John Foster Dulles." The same source told me that Dulles was afraid Americans would panic at the thought of aliens' appearing in spacecraft.

It is a little-known fact that the talented people who designed the space shuttle used hundreds of UFO photographs—many of them taken by McDonnell-Douglas personnel—in designing the spacecraft. No one is permitted to talk about this. Stonewalling of this type from the Pentagon, NASA, the CIA, and other areas of the government has made a lot of sane and rational folks doubt their leaders—not their eyesight.

Clearly, there is a strong public demand for further information about UFOs. New magazines on the subject seem to crop up every month. Millions of newspapers are sold through splashy coverlines that discredit UFOlogy. Whether the coverage is positive or negative, fair or biased, it calls the public's attention to the subject. Even articles with such titles as "UFOs and Other Nonsense" by scientists and scientific investigators often do more to attract attention to the UFOs than to discredit them.

From science fiction often springs reality. In recent years there has been an explosion of interest in UFOlogy. Such movies as *Close Encounters of the Third Kind* and *Star Wars* have met with record box-office sales; there is a renewed interest in television programs like "Star Trek" and "The Twilight Zone." No one has a monopoly or patent on the one absolute truth. On the contrary, a great many people are thinking and writing about the impossible and the unorthodox from the springboard of personal experience. I often wonder if that isn't where some of our science "fiction" writers get their creative insights.

I have personally spoken to more than fifty people who either saw, filmed, or boarded UFOs—airline pilots, professors, doctors, physicists, businessmen, students, and everyday individuals like you and me. None of them are the type to hallucinate. Many are the type, however, to keep their experiences quiet lest they be subjected to derision and scorn. I'm happy to say that things may be looking up for these people. The CIA is currently being sued for a UFO cover-up, which may prompt our government to become more open, and the United Nations is working to establish a separate agency to study UFOs.

Tauri has had something to say about this problem:

AP: A positive vote from the United Nations on the UFO project might have a very healing effect on the nations that go to make up the UN. Do you concur?

T: Let's put it this way. There are those who *search* for extraterrestrials, yes? There are those who talk *to* extraterrestrial intelligence, yes? And there are those nations who, when united in a project such as this one, can bring information forward to a public who have fear. This is my concern, as you know. *Allay* the fear is still the big number one project for the Ogatta group to impart to the channels we use. Isn't it marvelous that nations are now discussing "how much" to allocate for something that they did not believe *existed* not that long ago— and are still not sure! I think that's wondrous! I think that's progress. I think that's . . . very human. . . .

AP: That whole project would be advanced if one craft came down for all of them to see.

T: You'd be amazed at how many of them know how tangible they are. Same to be said in your scientific group: you'd be amazed at how many of them have been out on some of these "gattae," would you not? I think the important thing is that they are debating it at all . . . talking about it.

It has gone beyond the talking stages in France. The French National Space Committee, which corresponds roughly to our NASA, has recently allocated funds for UFO studies to a subsection called GEPAN. In the Soviet Union, "anomalous atmospheric phenomena" were analyzed in a scientific, statistical report published under the auspices of the prestigious Academy of Sciences. The United States seems to be dragging its feet.

Yet things are moving along. There are universities that are beginning to include UFOlogy in their curriculums. And, of course, there is always the hope that President Carter will make good on his original campaign promise.

Buckminster Fuller has a story in *I Seem to Be a Verb* that indirectly sheds light on the debate about whether or not money should be spent on UFO investigations. He tells of the astronomer who stands and looks up at the starry sky and wistfully remarks, "Sometimes I think we are alone. Sometimes I think we're not alone. In either case, the thought is quite staggering!" It *is* a staggering thought and—either way—the public deserves to know. The UFO phenomenon is the harbinger of major changes in the scientific outlook around the world. After all, things that do not fit into our present picture of reality can point the way to new knowledge, new departures, new conjectures about ourselves and about our Universe. We must be open to possibilities. As E.F. Schumacher says in his *Guide for the Perplexed*, "The modern world tends to be skeptical about everything that makes demands on man's higher faculties. But it is not at all skeptical about skepticism which demands hardly anything."

Much skepticism is fading where 2,181 cases of physical landing traces of UFOs from sixty-four countries are studied. There has been a statistical increase of these landing trace samples during the past thirty years, bringing the average from nineteen to the current ninety-six in a year. Weight calculations indicate that objects of eight to ten tons leave the resulting imprints and residue. They help dispel the notion that UFOs are merely "night lights in the sky."

Channeled information tells us that some UFOs do, in fact, exist. Only they are not "unidentified." They are spacecraft from other civilizations, some of them gattae from my friends, the Ogatta group. The ETI tell us that their "UFOs" use *light* for energy. Humans have used fossilized energy from the earliest known geological period. From this pre-Cambrian light we get coal, oil, and gas. But the ETI propel their gattae with light. Light is velocity (186,000 miles per second). Velocity is energy. Light, therefore, is energy. Einstein proved that mass equals energy in the great poem of this century, $E = mc^2$. He proved it with a big *bang*! He showed that matter converts to energy. We learn in particle physics that subatomic particles are not made of energy, they *are* energy. Subatomic interactions are interactions of energy with energy: the particle aspects existing for less than a millionth of a second. The human being is totally a composition of these ephemeral particles.

I wish to share some information that you will be able to verify if NASA ever opens its stonewalled files. It is a story about the moon, and it's far *more astounding* than the cosmic Watergate—it is cosmic Wonderment.

19

The Moon Story

ON MARCH 4, 1977, Dick and I were having dinner in a local restaurant when I leaned over and asked him if he heard any music. He didn't. I then said to him, "You are supposed to tell me how far the Moon is from the Earth, and how far Vesta is from the Earth. I don't know why, but that's the message that I seem to be getting."

That telepathic message from Tauri was the first one I got right without the use of words. This was made clear later that night when she talked to Dick, allowing the conversation to be taped.

T: She did very well with the message I sent to her tonight. That was the first time she got it 100 percent right.

D: How far is Vesta from here?

T: I told her that you are supposed to know that.

D: I know how far the Moon is, but not Vesta.

T: Then you can find out!

D: All right, I will. Tauri, whose music was playing that Greta could hear?

T: That was our music, and I had a reason for putting it into the message. Tonight I am going to tell you something very strange, but it is a fact. Do you know why we are on Vesta for the coming of the gattae?

D: You once told us it was a staging area.

T: We're on Vesta because Ogatta decided it was a better place for this way station than your Moon. And do you know that a lot of things were built up there by those from Ogatta? There are gorgeous, beautiful structures up there on your Moon. Do you know that a lot of your people in the NASA know that? Do you know that they had to be very careful in plotting where your spacecraft landed so as not to disturb them? And do you know that some of your astronauts know it? Do you know that under microscopy they have pictures of these structures? But noooobody on Earth knows that they were built by the beings on Ogatta for the coming of the gattae (until Ogatta decided he'd use Vesta). I am telling it to you tonight and it is my present to you.

D: Thank you, Tauri.

T: When she starts to talk and to write, maybe it would be a good thing to contact somebody who does know. Then it would be more di-gest-ible to the people who listen on your Planet Earth. Don't you think so?

D: I think so.

T: Maybe you should contact some of the people at your NASA and maybe you should talk to one or two of the astronauts because they know. And then when she speaks out on the coming of the gattae, these people might admit what *they* know too. They *know* but they never ever said anything. They took a secret oath, but they know. It didn't matter until now. Do you understand?

D: Yes. It is very important.

T: Bridges, and all kinds of things they built there. I know all about that. I was not there but I was on Ogatta and I know what they built there.

D: Bridges? What else did they build on the Moon?

T: All kinds of landing places and domes and things. And they are shiny and they are like, well, silvery, and they are beautiful. We don't have anything that fancy on Vesta, you know, because we didn't need it on Vesta.

D: Why did you need it on the Moon but not on Vesta?

T: I don't know why they had to do that up there, but there are lots of things about that Moon that nobody knows.

D: Can you tell me some of the other things?

T: [*Named just one and later took it off the tape.*] I tell you that they know and there are all kinds of records at the N-A-S-A, NASA!

D: That's in Houston.

T: I know. Houston. That's in one of your big states down there. Well, as long as you understand that the message that I gave to you tonight as a present is an important message, I'll repeat part of what is not on your tape! Your people at the NASA and a few of your astronauts should be pushed to give her validity when she starts to talk and to write. Let me tell you that it is a *fact* that they are completely con-vinced that the structures were not made by humans! Do you under-stand the significance of what I say to you? They know it was done by extraterrestrial beings, made by what they call "humanoids," and that is very important for you to think about.

After hearing this tape replayed, Dick and I stared at each other. One thing at a time, we agreed. First, Dick had to do all the research he could on Vesta. So, he set to work—and nearly drove me crazy in the process. For days he mumbled about "a.u.'s" which turned out to be astronomical units. I'd ask him to pass the salt and he'd say, "Did you know that the asteroid belt is 2.7 a.u.'s from the Sun?" When we were going to visit friends some distance away, and I asked how long it would take us to drive there, he looked through me and said, "Gret, Vesta lies approximately 250 million miles from the Sun, which makes it about 158 million miles from the Earth. Did you know that?"

No. I just wanted to know how long it would take to get to Boston.

One night I laughingly said that all his cross-referencing work (which went on every day and well into every night) did not bode well for our sex life. Would you believe that he actually answered, "Bode? Bode? Hey, do you know about the Titius Bode Law? It's an empirical, mathematical expression for the relative mean distances between the Sun and its planets." I gave up. My mind was on libido, and his was on albedo. "Albedo means power to reflect light and electromagnetic radiations, you know. The albedo rating of the Earth is 30 percent. How about that?"

When all Dick's research was done, however, the pertinent findings boiled down to just a couple of sentences. To wit: Vesta, which is the fourth minor planet, commonly called an asteroid, was discovered on March 29, 1807, by a German astronomer named Heinrich Olbers. Its diameter is 240 miles, approximately one-ninth the diameter of the Moon, which is 2,160 miles. Its albedo, or reflecting power, is *four times* that of the Moon.

How many times had Tauri mentioned the importance of light? How many times had she indicated—both in and out of Andrija Puharich's copper cage—that *light is energy*, and that energy will be needed to produce the loops which will power the spacecraft coming into our dimension?

His research completed, Dick watched me like a hawk, hoping that Tauri would take over the channel so that he could talk to her about his discoveries. He didn't have long to wait. In less than a "moon," Tauri came in with her husky, delicious, whispery voice to discuss that matter further.

T: You want to know why Ogatta originally planned to have the Moon as the way station. Is that your question, Dick?

D: Yes, it is, Tauri.

T: Well, to start with, the plan for the landing of the gattae started some time ago, as you know time. Structures were built, and bridges and domes, and places to land. I told you all of that. Do you know something rather curious? Do you know that only a few of the astronauts on your planet really understand *what* the Moon is, because they are the only ones who have seen the *whole* Moon? Don't you know that?

D: I know they circled the Moon before they landed.

T: That's right. Now, when you send telepathic messages, *time* as you know it and *distance* as you know it, do *not* have too much relativity. And, speaking of distance reminds me: Vesta is 241 miles in diameter, not 240!!

D: Britannica says 240, Tauri.

T: Huh. Look to earlier resources if you wish. Not important, not important. It's an ugly place anyway. What difference is one mile out there!!

(Five months later when we browsed through a book in the Library of Valuable Knowledge, printed in 1902, Dick and I noted Vesta: 241 miles in diameter.)

T: When you talk about the gattae, the distance and the time have a little more meaning. There has to be a way station, but the factor that was involved was not that of distance and not that of time. The important factor was of *light*. Light in your solar system. So then, it was decided, after all those beautiful structures were built, that the Moon had to be abandoned regardless of its wonderful light factor. There is more about the Moon that you would not know about. Everything stopped. Then came the choosing of Vesta. It's really not a very nice place, you know! But anyway, Vesta was chosen because of its light factor.

D: The light on Vesta is four times that of the Moon. The albedo rating of Vesta is four times that of the other asteroids and the Moon.

T: So you did a little homework, did you, Dick? Yes, I think you have to understand about the light factor. The albedo. I know that *that* is why we are on this dumb place, and I know that it probably would have been better to have staged it from the Moon, but we couldn't do that. All those gorgeous things up there, oh my goodness. All those things I told you about. Oh, yes, they have some pictures *buried* at your N-A-S-A, NASA!

D: Tauri, when you say the light is the biggest factor, I want to understand the significance. Do the gattae and other spacecraft generate energy from the light of the Sun?

T: Some. A good part of the energy comes from the loops, you know. The energy stones. Anyway, here we are on Vesta. I'll tell you something. They couldn't have used all the space you are so concerned with on the Moon anyway. So even though it's much bigger than Vesta, ten or even twelve times bigger—whatever—it didn't matter at all.

D: Where did the materials on the Moon come from with which to build all those beautiful domes and structures?

T: Ogatta! Only Ogatta. Only one structure is not from Ogatta! I *don't* want to talk about *it*.

D: All of the bridges, all the material used to build the bridges came from Ogatta?

T: The material is called lavahn and has no correlation to anything on Earth. Well, it looks a bit like silvery mother-of-pearl. And *everything* was transported from Ogatta by our gattae.

D: They were not teletransported by dematerialization?

T: No. They were brought by the gattae, and our "people" stayed there on that Moon while the structures were being built. A lot of them stayed there in the gattae but I didn't go. I was not there.

D: Tauri, can beings from Ogatta breathe on the Moon?

T: Those from Ogatta can breathe *any*where when they wear their feathers. Of course, there are places where they do not need their feathers at all. Like Vesta, ugly old place! It's hard for you to comprehend what that means, isn't it, dear Dick?

D: Well, I guess the feathers are the things that allow them to travel anywhere in the Cosmos.

T: *Any*where at all. They are not like humans, you know, not Ogattans! It takes a lot of doing to get to Ogatta, you know.

D: Tauri, can you give me an approximation in the Earth-time calendar when those buildings were constructed on the Moon?

T: In your "years," you mean?

D: Yes, please.

T: Not that long ago. You were on your ship. You were in a uniform on a ship at that time.

D: Why, that was in the years 1951 and '52. Thank you. I have one more question I have wanted to ask you. Is there any water on Ogatta?

T: Not as you know water which you *pour*. But there are *seas of moisture* which are equal to your water in *globes* all over Ogatta.

D: Can you explain what the globes are? What do you call them?

T: Our globes hold moisture as your flowers hold dew. And then, that moisture can be used in some ways as you use water, but more than that I cannot explain to you right now, okay? Oh, and we call them "brieta."

D: Okay, Tauri, and thank you very much. You have been most instructive. Perhaps you can tell me more about the brieta and seas of moisture at another time.

T: You did very well with the studies, you did very well indeed. Now I must go back out there.

D: Goodbye, Tauri.

The next night, Tauri returned to finish her incredible story. She permitted Dick to tape the session so that I could hear it, but cautioned him to erase it subsequently or she would "blow it up." Dick erased it. But first he took careful notes on why Ogatta left the Moon. . . .

Not all beings who watch Planet Earth have the same motives. Some feel strongly about Planet Earth's survival, but others do not care one way or the other. A very few would like to see Earth destroyed. Those from Ogatta not only choose to see her survive the holocaust that is to come, but plan to lend their technology to ease the transition. At the time that the Ogattans were building their structures on the Moon, another group from a civilization called Glosta was also putting up a structure. Their motive was less than altruistic toward our planet, and the structure had a purpose which boded ill for us. Ogatta recognized the structure and the motive. A pact was made for both civilizations to abandon the Moon. All existing structures were to stay intact. Both Ogatta and Glosta agreed that human beings are not doing the best possible job on their Earth Planet, but Ogatta wished to help repair the coming damage and Glosta wished to help Earth toward her own destruction. Tauri also told Dick that just because extraterrestrials communicated with us on

Earth, it did not necessarily mean they wanted to be helpful. A warning was once again issued to me to "know your voices and your music."

Some of the random notes of that session between Dick and Tauri include an item stating that these gleaming structures, with their shiny domes and silvery tracks, appear in NASA pictures! Tauri reiterated that both civilizations chose the Moon because of its light factor in our solar system. The Glosta structure, which looks like a huge triangle, is also on film in the NASA files. The purpose of the Glosta structure may not be told at this time, but I'm relieved to report that it is now a defunct operation. One last thing: Tauri would neither deny nor confirm Dick's questions about life on other planets in this solar system.

The session ended with the reminder that "twenty-plus civilizations" are concerning themselves with giving aid to our planet, by sharing their advanced technology with us. Those of the Ogatta jorpah are pleased with the progress made on Vesta toward the coming of the gattae and other spacecraft. Tauri gave us one final fascinating insight. She stated that humans should never forget that love is an energy as well as an emotion, and that "human beings respond very well to love."

That night Dick and I slept very little. We talked a great deal about what we had learned, but we agreed to say absolutely nothing about the Moon story. We maintained our silence until a year later, almost to the day, when I spoke of it in a lecture delivered to a standing-room-only crowd in the Whig Hall Senate Chamber at Princeton University.

Now you know about it, too. Does the "you" include someone from NASA—an astronaut, perhaps—who will speak out with me? I wonder.

20

"Land of Ices"

MIND OVER MATTER:

THE FRONTIERS OF PHYSICS CONFERENCE

Reykjavik, Iceland, November 12, 1977—At a five day meeting here, "The Frontiers of Physics Conference" scientists from the United States, France, Great Britain, Denmark and Sweden have presented laboratory data confirming the role of the human mind in influencing physical events. For the first time, experimental physicists have agreed with their theorist colleagues that the findings on the workings of the mind can possibly be integrated into a coherent theory of the universe.

THIS RELEASE defined the purpose and conclusion of the Frontiers of Physics Conference, which was attended by forty representatives from the scientific, technological, and industrial fields. The conference was a forum for the presentation of new data collected through experimentation around the globe over the past five years.

Symposiums were established so that consciousness research and physics research could blend. The data included carefully documented scientific evidence which upset the long-established claim by physicists that human mentation cannot affect large-scale physical experimentation.

Noting that an actual demonstration, rather than a mere postulation, of mentation had been given, the release went on to say: "One psychically gifted participant stunned Icelandic newspaper and television reporters by causing stainless steel spoons to bend measurably within seconds without physical contact."

I was that "gifted particpant."

The invitation to the Frontiers of Physics Conference had been extended to Dick and me as "industrialists." (We are both presidents of our respective companies.) We had planned to be inconspicuous, silent observers, but our plans were unexpectedly changed, and—as frequently happens to me—the change was due to transportation problems.

Cancelled flights, stalled traffic, derailed trains, and missed arrivals and departures invariably trigger psychic activity for me, and our trip to Reykjavik was no exception. Dr. Andrija Puharich, who was scheduled to chair the conference, missed flights in two European countries, and as a result, arrived at Reykjavik's Loftleider Hotel two days later than planned. In those intervening—and seemingly interminable—forty-eight hours, a polarization started to develop between the scientists and the "outsiders," (which included Dick and me).

We had been invited to hear these distinguished physical scientists report on their latest research into psi phenomena. Yet the undercurrent was clearly one of asking why "we"—the nonscientists—were at a "closed" conference and wondering how freely "they"—the scientists—could speak.

One reason for the conference, and our invitation to it, had been to narrow the gulf between the scientific and nonscientific communities; but the way things were going, that gulf could only get wider. Then for no apparent reason, I found myself involved in an unexpected and unusually intense spate of metal-bending. Twenty-three spoons in one day at breakfast, lunch, and dinner!

It happened at the table during meals, in anterooms and corridors during coffee breaks. I felt then, as I do now, that this unprecedented spectacle was exquisitely orchestrated by the Ogatta group, for I have never believed for even a moment that I can bend metal. (And if the truth be known, I'd be delighted never to be involved in any metal-bending demonstrations again.) At this point, however, I must admit that it was an exhilarating experience, and it did prove to be the key factor in breaking the ice with some of the more conservative and hostile scientists. (It may have also depleted the Loftleider Hotel's silverware supply—I extend belated apologies!)

Some of the scientists present had never seen anyone bend metal strictly by mind power or mentation. Some, in their almost messianic zeal to question anything that did not occur under laboratory conditions, witnessed the bending of metal but refused to acknowledge it publicly. Others hung back, waiting for someone else to admit to seeing the phenomenon before discussing their own experiences. Even then, most of these cautious creatures would only talk off the record! All of the scientists we met were eager to protect their hard-earned credentials in the academic and/or scientific community, not to mention their hard-earned funding.

Starting with our noon meal on the first day, and at every meal thereafter, various groups of conference participants witnessed the metal-bending phenomenon. Most of them took home a sample of a "control" (i.e., normal) spoon and a bent one. One delightful scientist from Denmark drew the outlines of a couple of spoons on a paper napkin both before and after the bending and then pocketed four spoons wrapped in the "control" napkin.

Iceland, with its volcanoes, hot springs, and lava pits, has a stark beauty. Situated at the top of the world (or, as Tauri said, "Living in the 'Land of Ices' "), it is a land of hardworking, handsome, solid, spiritual citizens. Dick and I fell in love with the unexpectedly mild climate and the gentle and gracious people.

The first night we studied the format and agenda of the conference. We were impressed to see that there would be no media coverage of any kind at the closed sessions. The scientists, humanists, and industrialists were gathered to share scientific research data, and to see how they would effect sociological and industrial change. The industrialists recognized that funding for various projects was, and is, desperately needed by the scientific community. But the main emphasis of the meeting was to be on perception data, psychokinesis, theory, application, and strategy within the psi phenomena field.

At 9 P.M. on November 6, our Icelander host Thorsteinn Jonsson-Ulfsstodus opened the conference. The first meeting took place the next morning. Andrija, who was to have led off the program, had still not arrived, so the meeting opened with the presentation of a paper by a highly respected laser physicist. He was followed by a well-known author. The names Geller, Girard, and Swann came up frequently, since many of the physicists who attended the conference had worked on the laboratory testing of these three psychics. Papers on the quantum of psi phenomena were presented, as was a report on a psychotronic conference in Japan. In addition, we heard in-depth theories on the effects of volition on experimental apparatus and on sonic emission studies.

At first the speakers seemed extremely uptight—at least that was the impression among us nonscientists. After Andrija arrived, he was told that "the polarization ended when metal started to bend." I'd like to think that was so. It was certainly true that by the time Andrija got there, the entire group was interfacing on many levels. The initial reserve, tension, and suspicion had evaporated, and everyone was communicating comfortably with everyone else.

Once the conference was in full swing, the Icelandic press became interested in what was being discussed behind closed doors. It was known that several Icelanders were making presentations, among them engineer Gudmandur Einarsson, biochemist Th. Thorsteinsson and author Thorsteinn Gudjonsson. (Other Icelanders were present but had gone to great lengths to conceal their identities from the press.)

After repeated attempts by reporters to find out what was happening, it was finally agreed that a press conference would be held in Andrija's suite on the last day of the conference. Several scientists, physicists, and researchers were selected to be interviewed.

When the reporters from the Reykjavik papers and the national television station arrived, however, the majority of the interviewees were out on a sightseeing tour—the only one of the entire conference! Once again transportation problems were the factor that triggered what was to follow.

Andrija was anxiously pacing up and down in his suite when the media representatives arrived. With him was Christopher Bird, author of *The Secret Life of Plants* and *The Divining Hand*. My room was just down the hall but confused by the profusion of look-alike doors, I unwittingly wandered into the suite. Andrija's face lit up, and he rushed to introduce me, remarking that in the course of the conference I had bent metal for almost everybody in attendance. This fascinated the reporters and they began to interview me.

I answered their questions politely but declined to bend metal for them. Instead, I tried to entertain the reporters by talking about some of our lighter observations of the Iceland experience. I was sure that the busload of conference participants would return at any moment, and it was supposed to be their news conference—certainly not mine.

Time passed, and the press grew increasingly impatient. We were informed that television was limited in Iceland. Reykjavik had only three 15-minute segments of news—at 9 A.M., 12 noon, and 8 P.M. The 8 P.M. prime-time newscast was, of course, the most popular; it was also the one on which the television reporters hoped to air this story.

As we sat there making conversation and watching the clock, coffee and tea were brought into the suite. What finally ensued can best be told in the rather ungrammatical translation of the lead item on Iceland's 8 P.M. TV news on Saturday, November 12. It was sent to me by one of the Icelander writers.

The program opened with a still shot of me holding a bent teaspoon on my open palm, as the anchor newsman Omar Ragnarsson said:

Can flowers be spoken to? Can diseases be healed, and can spoons bend all by the power of the mind alone? Has the human mind access to an inexplicable power which can remove ills from the living body and find hidden objects in the bowels of the earth? At a press conference held at Hotel Loftleider at two o'clock today, an American lady named Greta Woodrew showed to reporters cases of her abilities in this field by bending two teaspoons in their presence. The reporters who came to the press conference at the hotel today were rather incredulous when they were shown two teaspoons, one of which had been bent by Mrs. Woodrew by holding it in her hand and rubbing it gently before the eyes of forty scientists from several countries who have been discussing, in a number of sessions during the whole week, phenomena that belong to the verge or frontier of physics. Truly, these events have occurred under the strictest control of the scientists, and a number of such phenomena have now received the recognition of the scientists both on the western and eastern side of the Iron Curtain. When the reporters asked Greta Woodrew to repeat the experiment, the foreign scientist present who had announced the conference said that it would depend upon the positive attitude and easy mood of the persons present whether results could be expected. But the following pictures were taken at the press conference today:

The television picture showed two teaspoons that were given to me before the eyes of the reporters. I took one of the teaspoons, let it balance on my fingertip, and rubbed it gently with another finger. And lo! slowly and gradually the teaspoon bent! When it was placed by the side of the other teaspoon on the table, the difference could clearly be seen.

Remarking on the very positive attitude of the Frontiers of Physics conferees, the newsman went on to say:

At the conference, Greta had succeeded in bending a teaspoon which lay on a table just by knocking lightly *under* the table, and without touching the spoon on the upper side at all. This was judged to be very important by the scientists. When coffee was served at the press conference today, Greta said that the atmosphere was better than she had expected, *and she placed her hand under the table beneath one of the saucers where a teaspoon lay on its edge.* The reporters could hardly believe their own eyes when the teaspoon began to bend, while Greta rubbed and knocked gently on the lower surface of the table. In this picture we can see the difference between the spoons that lay on the table when this happened.

Greta Woodrew says of herself that she cannot explain the energy which enables her to bend metals but she feels that something unknown stands behind her efforts. At the press conference today we ultimately met some highly reputable scientists from both east and west of the Atlantic who are active in this kind of research. At the conference they tried to decide how the relativity theory of Einstein and Max Planck's quantum theory could be adjusted to describe the phenomena that are now on the verge of physics!

As a case of explicable phenomena from the viewpoint of physics, a thin rail of wire was shown to reporters which was made of a mixture of titanium and nickel which seems to have a "memory"; this property of the metal is used in making antennae for spacecraft. When the rail is given its first form at a certain temperature—say at a very high or low grade on our everyday scale and wrapped up at room temperature, it can then take back its first form again. (The metal is a member of a new class of materials known as Shape Memory Effect alloys. Uri Geller has "destroyed the memory" in the past. Greta "destroyed" the memory today by simply touching it!) Now we see the rail as it looked today.

Indeed, few things seem impossible when we enter these fields. Thus the mind-benders, if we may say so, bent a support from titanium which is being used in the Concorde. We are told that this was being done under stringent scientific control. And indeed, no observation indicated that for this act any force had been applied except the inexplicable force of the mind which the reporters came to witness at the press conference.

Let me clarify quickly what the "rail of wire" was. The mixture of titanium and nickel, Nitinol, was developed at the Naval Surface Weapons Center in Maryland. The unique Shape Memory Effect (SME) characteristic of this alloy is used in component applications aboard ships, aircraft, submarines, and space vehicles. It also has a wide variety of industrial and biomedical applications. The demonstration is simple: you coil the wire around a finger or a pencil. Remove the wire, which is at room temperature, from the pencil and, with a match, gently heat it. As the heat is applied, the wire straightens out as its internal crystal structure changes. Metallurgically speaking, the structure has changed from "martensite" to "austenite." Once curled around my finger, it sprang back to the original shape as anticipated, but then it began to arc and curve *again* to the amazement of reporters, scientists, and most of all—me.

When the story of my metal-bending broke in the press, I was amazed and delighted that the Icelandic people made the equation between the energy used for metal-bending and the energy used for healing. They *are* the same. Scores of people showed up in the lobby of our hotel seeking help. Requests to visit and aid the ill, the dying, the incurable, and the congenitally deformed poured in. Dick and I were scheduled to leave the next morning, but once again there were transportation difficulties, and once again they triggered psychic activity. It was to be more than twenty-four hours before we could board a plane for home. One of our Icelander hosts, Gudmundur Einarsson, a scientist and engineer with a strong understanding and sympathy for the needs of his compatriots, asked that I go to the hospital to help "heal" in the dying ward. I readily agreed.

There are so many stories that could be recounted of my experiences the day after that newscast! The one I love best occurred after we returned from the hospital and found a mother and her 15-year-old daughter waiting for us in the hotel lobby. The girl, whose name was Sigurbjorg, had long, curly blonde hair and the face of an angel. She had also been deaf since birth, a fact to which Gudmundur sadly attested, having known the family since before she was born.

Sigurbjorg, who rarely watched television, had for some reason felt "compelled" to lip-read the evening news that night. When my picture flashed on the screen, just before the announcer began his report, Sigurbjorg jumped out of her chair, pointed to me, and cried out, in her native tongue, "She's the one! Shes the one who can make me hear!"

As the mother told the story, I could see that there was to be no ignoring or arguing with this child. As the two of them stood there in the hotel lobby and looked at me pleadingly, my heart went out to them. It had been a hectic nonstop day, but I motioned them to an elevator, grabbed two spoons from a tray that was standing outside the dining room (why did I do that?) and went upstairs.

The girl, who spoke no English, appeared nervous at first, but smiles and reassuring pats are universal, and in a few moments we were friends. Working by instinct, I walked around behind her so that she could not see me, and, after some concentrating, I took the spoons and pressed one to each ear. Then I clanged them together behind the girl. Her head cocked quizzically to the right, where the spoons were. Still outside of her vision range, I clanged them on the left side of her head and one spoon transcribed an arc in my hand. The girl's eyes widened and, as I clanged the spoons for the third time, her eyes flooded with tears. Sigurbjorg said to her mother in Icelandic, "I hear something." The girl, her mother, Dr. Einarsson, Dick, and I unabashedly wept with joy.

I handed Sigurbjorg the two spoons and instructed her mother to tell her not to let anyone touch them but herself, and to place them each morning and evening on the front part of her ears keeping them there until the cool feeling wore off.

Suddenly I heard myself addressing our guests in Icelandic, a language I've never studied. I directed them to a verse in Corinthians II (which I have never read), giving the chapter, verse, and page number in their Icelandic Bible. Dick went into another room and got a Bible. Gudmundur opened it to the right page, and I told Sigurbjorg and her mother that this particular passage would have a great influence on the girl's future ability to hear—if only she could understand its meaning. The mother seemed to find some meaning in the verse, but to this day I still do not understand it myself. It was not until later that the realization hit us all that I had expressed myself in a language I don't know.

One month later, Dick and I received a Christmas card from the mother who wrote that Sigurbjorg had "heard music." Again, we wept with joy. Unfortunately, in April 1978 we received a letter from the mother, telling us that "the spoons have stopped working." I instructed her to send them back to me—which she did—and after a unique healing session with a sensitive friend and Dick standing by, the spoons arced again, this time in the hands of my friend, a nonbeliever in metal-bending. We sent them back to Iceland and have yet to hear the results. My thoughts often go out to Sigurbjorg as I wait and hope for the best.

During the entire Frontiers of Physics Conference and the unplanned extra time in Iceland, I was unbearably thirsty. I consumed huge quantities of water, but my thirst seemed to be unquenchable. Sometimes my mouth was so cotton-dry that I literally could not speak. Oddly enough, I did not eliminate this water in the normal manner. Tauri explained it:

Her body absorbs it and will not give it back. You don't have a real grasp on energy fields . . . very real energies. She is thirsty and drinks a great deal and retains it because her body needs the moisture. You should push water on her. Not coffee, no! Water—pure water. Rain water. When we use our channel in things like the bending of metal, we *use* part of what is in her, and that something is moisture. So yes, she drinks the liquids and they do not pass through her system because her water-based body needs the replacement. Nature does not make mistakes in these things.

Our final hours in Iceland were a whirlwind of activity. As a result of that lead item in the telecast, I was recognized every place I went, and Dick and I were bombarded with questions. No one scoffed. The Icelandic people just wanted to talk about and understand the phenomena. I was even offered the opportunity to settle in Iceland and continue my work.

By the time the story of my metal-bending hit the front pages of the Icelandic press, we were back in the quiet of our Connecticut home. I'm just as glad! The *Dagbladid* ran a front-page picture of my hand holding a bent spoon, with two control spoons next to it on the table. The article inside was accompanied by another picture of me, taken during the interview, and had an accurate and very positive account of the proceedings. The *Morgunbladid,* the most widely read paper in Iceland, went all out. They ran two pictures and a full-page story. The "Dag" subsequently ran two more articles. Like all the other articles, they exaggerated certain claims and misquoted me (perhaps that's par for the course with the press), but in general they were favorable, fair, and completely openminded.

I had a letter from one Icelander friend who said that such publicity had never before been accorded to "this type of happening." I know that I have never before been the object of such publicity. It made me most uncomfortable at the time. I actually squirmed when I read the section of the newscast transcript where I was described as being famous for decades. Silent, yes. Famous, no!

A paper issued by Thorsteinn Gudjonsson, "The Creation of a Progressive Psi-Field in Iceland," noted my contribution to the conference that had brought us to Iceland in the first place.

"The results of the physicists at the conference, important as they were, could only have been brought together by such enthusiastic and harmonical meeting as the Frontiers of Physics assembly was, from the beginning to the end. The factor of prime importance for the whole fortunate development was, beyond question, the presence of Ms. Greta Woodrew of Conn. USA at the conference. Being a dynamic personality herself, Ms. Greta Woodrew recently discovered her mind-metal-bending ability, and this power happily continued to manifest itself during the conference."

The Frontiers of Physics Conference was a success for any number of reasons. First of all, it brought together authorities from a variety of disciplines to exchange ideas and, perhaps, open each other's minds. Physicists, humanitarians, industrialists, scientists, psychics had the chance to exchange ideas and compare problems, not only in group meetings, but on a one-to-one, first-name basis. Everyone came away with new friends, new ideas, and, above all, new perspectives.

It provided the backdrop for me to express the urgent need for a new vocabulary for both the scientific and the psychic communities to communicate comfortably. We need theories to transcend the current possibilities, to expand—and challenge—the wealth of factual information we now have, and, ultimately, to enable us to participate in the tomorrow of mankind today.

The events that surrounded my metal-bending were gratifying. The spontaneous response of the Icelandic population—open-minded, questioning, thoughtful—showed me that not everyone in the world is quick to reject new possibilities. The Icelanders' very warm response gives me the hope that our planet *will* be responsive and receptive when the gattae come. I risk the prediction that many *will* be—in the hope that it might be a spur for many others who *could* be.

Still another thing that the conference brought home to me was the need to keep chipping away at the rigid barriers that too many scientists have constructed against psi phenomena. There are none so blind as scientists who cling to the scientific dogma of the past.

I will never forget an episode that occurred on the second morning of the conference. A widely published researcher, renowned for his laboratory work with Uri Geller in the testing of metal-bending, categorically stated that he had *never* seen metal bend. He and a female physicist selected three identical spoons that nested perfectly one inside the other, and asked me to bend one of them. I suggested that I not touch any of the spoons and asked the woman to hold them instead.

"Shrink!" I commanded mentally, not really taking myself seriously. One spoon subsequently became smaller than the others. Two other people—a professor/scientist and a physicist—were standing nearby and watched it happen.

"*Now* can you say that you saw metal bend?" I asked the researcher.

In spite of the fact that he had selected the spoons himself, he replied, "Well, this is a hallway not a laboratory. It was not done under proper scientific conditions."

"*Did* you see metal bend?" I asked vehemently.

"Well, no," was his answer. "I only saw it shrink."

Naturally he never mentioned this event in any of his research papers, nor would he commit his observations to paper (on or off the record) for me.

When the world was big, men could afford to be small. Today, the world is small, so men must be big. I look back at that episode with amusement, but it was not really amusing.

Traditional and unreceptive scientists have given me many moments of anxiety and personal turmoil. Canon John Rossner summed it up succinctly in one of his general bulletins: "Neither professional skeptics nor credulous persons are emotionally suited to the responsibilities of psychic research. Equilibrium is required for a fair and open-minded approach in any scientific field. In parapsychology today it is not a matter of 'believers' versus 'unbelievers' or of the 'rational' versus the 'irrational.' It is really only a matter of knowledge versus ignorance of the results obtained from over 40 years of well-controlled laboratory research."

The final message that I took away from the Reykjavik Conference was a renewed hope that the gap between various disciplines will be closed. This hope was rekindled by Dr. Olivier Costa de Beauregard, Director of Research at the Centre National de la Recherche Scientifique in Paris. This wonderful man, who specializes in relativistic and quantum mechanical theory, is among the most highly respected men in his field today. I wanted to bend a spoon for him very much, because I was curious to see what his response would be.

Dick and I sat with Dr. de Beauregard at a luncheon on November 7. Identical coffee spoons were laid between us by the waiter and apparently the time was right. We sat facing each other, talking while waiting for our soup, when suddenly I felt compelled to lean *under* the table and tap its underside. When the first spoon arced, tears came into Dr. de Beauregard's eyes. Who but the biggest researcher in the field would be unafraid to attest to what he saw without any discussion about scientific conditions, laboratory instruments, and the like?

I am forever indebted to Dr. de Beauregard for his enthusiasm and for his signed testimony, in the form of a letter to me, stating what he observed that day.

"She tapped underneath the table saying with insistence, 'Get up! Get up!' and the spoons bent!" he wrote. "The spoons were continuously under observation. The motion was fast and almost as directly visible as the motion of the long hand of a watch. The bend of both spoons is large, and occurred in a matter of minutes. Both spoons are presently in my possession, together with three test-ones which fit almost exactly together while the two other ones definitely do *not* fit with those three. The phenomena has been as obvious as that of a spoon falling to the ground through gravity. *This is more than I was prepared to believe when I came to consider psi phenomena, as a theoretical physicist."* [The italics are mine.]

Who better than Dr. de Beauregard could understand Neils Bohr, father of atomic physics, when he wrote that "there is no hope of advance in science without a paradox." Dr. Thomas Kuhn, in his widely respected work *The Structure of Scientific Revolutions*, aptly summarizes the problem that scientists encounter when the framework under which they practice their professions no longer meets all the needs. He states that "new and unsuspected phenomena are repeatedly uncovered by scientific research. Produced by a game played under one set of rules, their assimilation requires the elaboration of another set." The elaboration of this other set of rules is what he terms a "scientific revolution." He points out that after going through the difficulty of such a revolution, the scientists then find themselves responding to a different world.

Because paradoxes were acknowledged, science made an important advance in Reykjavik, and I was proud to have played a part in its progress. Nevertheless, there is still a strong need for integrated research into a multidimensional model of what I call the PSIence of consciousness.

Five select and erudite papers on experimental and theoretical explorations into the nature of consciousness have recently been released under the title *The Iceland Papers*. This book is a direct result of the conference and copies are to be placed in every major university library around the globe. Brian David Josephson, Nobel Prize winner for Physics 1973, wrote the foreword. I am proud to be mentioned in the acknowledgements for my "indefatigable role in Reykjavik." I am doubly pleased to have been coupled with Buckminster Fuller in that acknowledgment.

The Reykjavik Conference was a beginning. There is still much to learn. There is much to impart and share as well. Unfortunately, few grants, little academic recognition, and no public backing or government monies are available to facilitate the learning, the imparting, the sharing. For this reason we have set up the Space Technology and Research Foundation, Inc. (S.T.A.R.). The foundation is the recipient of all honorariums from my lectures and public appearances as well as monies from the sale of this book.

Relating to the world as we view it through our five normal senses, Thomas Kuhn stated, "Sensory experience is both fixed and neutral . . . and theories are simply manmade interpretations of given data. Questions about retinal imprints or about the consequence of particular laboratory manipulations presuppose a world already perceptually and conceptually subdivided in a certain way."

When Albert Einstein revealed his $E=mc^2$ formula, he reconstituted the three-dimensional world of man's five senses to include a fourth dimension—time/space. The areas of extrasensory perception (ESP) and psychokinesis (PK) provide an entry to this fourth dimension beyond man's "normal" senses. The scientific community—quantum and subatomic data notwithstanding—demands further evidence of this mind/matter link. Many respected scientists around the world are anxious to research this phenomenon but lack serious funding to do so.

I consider it vital that researchers get the encouragement and the funding they need because I believe, with St. Thomas Aquinas, that "The slenderest knowledge that may be obtained of the highest things is more desirable than the most certain knowledge obtained of lesser things."

21

Going Outward on a Slide of Light

AT THE TIME the Destiny Screen was rolled for me and I saw the Scenario so graphically painted, I wanted to weep for humanity. But there is no time to weep, just time to prepare. Tauri has reiterated, "If the message is to go out, it must go out in many ways. Remember that people fear most what they do not understand. The unknown factor is what makes people frightened. Conquer fear, conquer failure."

The unknown factor is how it all began. Our astronomers have postulated and theorized our beginnings with the "Big Bang." They have traced the birth of our solar system to 4.6 billion years ago. Several millennia later came life. Once when Dick and I were flying between Sydney, Australia, and Bali, Indonesia, my Destiny Screen rolled to give me a glimpse of the world's beginnings:

In the very beginning of time, the first living creatures came out of the sea. They were deeply affected by Moon. Moon-tide left its impact on the structure of animals and life. The tide went out and the animals were stranded on the beaches and on land. The tide came in and the animal was able to go back to the water . . . affected by the Moon. Yes, all of us are affected more by *lunar* than by *solar*.

We really do not know the full impact of lunar vibrations upon mankind. But we do know that there are significant statistical correlations between the energy increases from a full Moon and emotional disturbances among those confined to mental institutions. Although we can't explain the physiological effects of lunar tidal vibrations on human beings, at the time of a full Moon (the astronomers call it *syzygy*) there is an increase in the birth rate. There is excessive bleeding. There are outbreaks of violence recorded on police blotters around the world. There seems to be an increase in individual metabolism rates, as well as an increase in tensions and anxieties.

We also know that the human body is almost three-quarters water, and like any body of water, it must respond to the increased influence of heightened tidal pulls and electromagnetic effects. I have read that the creation of a body is always a chain reaction that, once begun, runs through various periods to an end. We can readily observe this phenomenon in all living things around us. The Earth is a living thing. It is entering another period in its chain reaction.

Planet Earth appears to be on the verge of Nature's cleansing—Nature's holocaust. Areas that are icy cold may turn tropically warm—and vice versa—in a matter of minutes. Earthquakes and volcanic eruptions will produce massive tidal activity and change the land mass, as we now know it. Instantaneous changes could occur, and there is a strong possibility of a polar flip—a shift of the earth on its axis—around the turn of the century. One archeologist, working with drill core samples and artifacts, postulates that the earth has already reversed magnetic fields 177 times.

Which areas are safe and which are not? Instincts coupled with judgment warns me that coastal areas can be altered drastically on both the eastern and western seaboards. Earthquakes will trigger major shifts, and we face the possibility of the Great Lakes meeting the Gulf of Mexico in one last horrendous change.

Simultaneously, we will be facing "man's inhumanity to man" on a broad range of fronts. What will make these situations different from similar ones that have occurred in the past will be their convergence at the very time that we will be facing Nature's holocaustic cleansing. I hope we will wake up to this realization and direct all of our efforts to meeting the transitional challenges. To dissipate our energies in any other way would be self-destructive. The phrase "man's inhumanity to man" haunts me and prods me into wondering if man is the actual cause of some of the holocaustic changes. Can he be the cause of the changes of which the Ogatta group spoke?

Glance at your daily paper, listen to the radio, watch the news on television. You can't fail to see the turmoil that is going on all over the world. There are few news items that do not give pause for reflection. In Europe and the Middle East, terrorists make their political statements by killing and maiming innocent people. In South America, kidnappings and hostage-taking are routine occurrences. In Africa, rebellion and repression—not to mention disease and starvation—keep entire populations at the mercy of both man and nature. Crucial strains in some of the major cities in our own country have already started to show.

From every continent and every country, the horror stories pour in—bombings, mass murders, guerrilla attacks, political prisoners beaten and tortured, epidemics, blights, and crop failures that result in the starvation of millions. The list is endless. All over the globe there are wars, political crises, and natural disasters that are affecting millions of human beings.

To add to our woes, we can expect an increase in the world population of 50 percent by the end of this century, the overwhelming numbers in the underdeveloped or Third World countries. These areas already harbor 800 million people who are plagued by malnutrition, illiteracy, diseases, high infant death rates, and a miserable life expectancy, a people whose standard of living is so low that Robert McNamara, president of the World Bank, described it as "below any rational definition of human decency."

But our global dangers are by no means limited to overpopulation. The two superpowers, the United States and the U.S.S.R., confront each other with huge arsenals of nuclear weapons. One false move could spell disaster for large segments of both countries' populations. And because of increasing distrust of the policies of either— or both—of these nations, many smaller nations are trying to achieve a nuclear capability of their own, thus geometrically increasing the danger of a nuclear conflict.

Another grave, but often unrecognized, global danger is the concept of unlimited growth, on which our modern economy is based. Our entire system of life is rooted in that concept, our business and government tailored to support it. But do we have infinite resources to achieve this infinite growth? When the first pictures of the Earth were flashed back to us from the Apollo Moon shot, I didn't see any highways or skyways from the outside bringing in the resources that are essential, if this inexhaustible need is to be supplied. The Planet

Earth appeared to be on its own. There cannot be infinite growth in a finite world. A *finite* planet does not have *infinite* resources!

The grim truth, as stated in a Club of Rome report issued in the early 1970s, is that all of our resources are finite, and they are all being expended at an extremely rapid rate. The theme of the Club's report: Nature cannot be counted on indefinitely to support an industrial system like the one we now have.

Today, almost a decade later, we are finally being forced to face up to some of the predicted shortages. And here in the United States we must also contend with increased competition from other nations to tap these fast disappearing resources.

Foremost on the list of our country's dwindling resources is petroleum. An article in the April 1979 issue of *New Age* magazine made the following statement:

Modern industrial agriculture, productive as it might be, sits on the shaky foundations of high energy consumption and environmental exhaustion. It now takes 80 gallons of gasoline to raise one acre of corn in this country. If American methods were applied worldwide, 80 percent of all energy would go to raising food. In addition, pumping in oil-based chemicals overwhelms the life in the soil and turns it into a dead medium for more and more petroleum products. The impacted land then becomes prone to erosion, costing valuable topsoil and carying the chemicals into lakes, streams, and seas, polluting our waterways.

The United Nations Food and Agricultural Organization expects the world food demand to rise above the 1978 level by about 44 percent by 1985 and by 112 percent by the year 2000. In other words, the world faces the staggering challenge of *doubling* its food production in twenty years. Can it be done? I fear that we will not even come close.

Modern industrial agriculture—the same mass production methods employed in the North American food-producing areas—is the current method of meeting these rapidly rising world needs. What will happen if our fossil fuel supplies run out or become so costly that it is prohibitive to use them for food production? Will a substitute means be found? Or will we face starvation on a worldwide basis? The fight for food when threats of famine are imminent could well become a prime example of man's inhumanity to man.

Petroleum is currently the basis for all our industrialization. As the Third World countries move to upgrade their economies and raise their standards of living, a global race for the world's dwindling oil supplies has ensued. The result? A series of staggering price inflations that is threatening bankruptcy to all but a handful of oil producers and industrialized giants. Unless—and until—a substitute is developed to provide the energy the world wants, and needs, we are in the grip of still another potential catastrophe. If modern industry were to falter—or fail—in its search for a replacement for oil, chaos would quickly result. A fight for the available but inadequate supplies could also become another example of man's inhumanity to man.

In our effort to find relief from the oil shortage we have developed a nuclear capacity for powering steam generators. Unfortunately, this development could well represent a grave danger to humanity. One report states that 65 percent of the nuclear reactors are located in seismically active areas. This does not mean that an earthquake *will* rupture the boilers that house the nuclear reactors. But it does mean that there is always the possibility that this *could* happen. In recognition of this possibility, the Nuclear Regulatory Commission on March 13, 1979, closed five atomic plants. Prophetically, a mild quake occurred shortly thereafter near the closed Maine-Yankee plant at Wiscasset, Maine with the epicenter within fifteen miles of the nuclear reactors.

Side effects of a too-rapid use of new discoveries also plague the medical and pharmaceutical world. Iatrogenic diseases—those caused by administration of man-made substances—have risen dramatically. What is used as a preventative for one disease is frequently discovered to be the cause of yet another disease a few years later. Man's inhumanity to man once again?

Changes. We must look to changes which have already begun: weather changes, planetary changes and discoveries, changing plate tectonics, growing season changes, social, economic and political changes, mental and physical changes. We are all in motion, in transition: the Earth around the Sun, the Sun around the galaxy, the galaxy around the Universe. As we move, the "living" conditions and vibrations affecting Planet Earth change. Changes have occurred before. Changes continue to occur. Change is the meaning of the term "New Age." In a new age, the path that the solar system takes around the Milky Way galaxy changes, and requires new vibrations to maintain its balance in this new orbit. Since the words "vibration" and "energy" can be used interchangeably for our purpose, all the planets and life forms in the solar system must adjust to these changed energies that will accompany this step into the New Age. It is these changed energies that trigger "Nature's plan," and probably excite "man's inhumanity to man." Those in the Ogatta jorpah have stated unequivocally: "Despite what man can do to man . . . and Nature's plan . . . there are those civilizations out there in the Cosmos who believe that Planet Earth is worth helping in its time of great adjustments."

Those in the Ogatta jorpah have evolved to a much higher level of consciousness. What separates beings in the Universe is not space but consciousness: the ability to handle additional and heightened vibrations. Those of the Ogatta group are going to share their universal knowledge with us—with you. The members of the Ogatta group will be able to point the direction and be among those to guide us into the new age—the Age of Aquarius about which our young people have been singing.

All new ages have altered man's way of life and this one will be no different. Since change causes trauma, all of us will be better able to handle the changes and inherent stresses if we are aware of *what* is occurring *while* it is happening. Fear of the unknown is man's greatest fear. We are in a transition period in our planet's evolution, and because we are always weakest in transition, we must be armed with the proper ammunition for survival. This is an unstable time historically, climatically, geologically, astronomically, socially, economically, politically. Those of the Ogatta group contribute insights and answers to many of the questions that echo all around us. And as I've said before, they will arrive in craft which our media refers to as UFOs but which they call "gattae."

We have been privy to phenomena unexplainable in scientific terms, for our technology on Planet Earth is not really very advanced. Most of it is less than two hundred years old. Would any reader over the age of forty have believed that a man would walk on the Moon or that a Skylab could be launched, if he were told these things prior to World War II? Not likely. Outer space was a term that used to appear only in science fiction; but today's young people have less trouble considering mind-stretching possibilities. Not only have they witnessed the conquest of outer space, they are not as bogged down as the members of the older generation, who have a vested interest in the status quo and are not eager to contemplate changes. Every time I lecture at a university, I meet students who have had stirring psychic experiences which defy what we currently consider to be natural law. When the mind bends metal, they are deeply touched by the sight. When they hear about the Ogatta group, they too want to understand the why and the how of the technologies to be shared and learned and used by all of us in the not-so-distant future.

Who can say what inventions will emanate from the grand-children and great-grandchildren of today's youth? Is it possible to envision the wonders they might unleash in science and the arts, in technology and ideology? Probably not. We can only stretch our imaginations. This is the wondrous thing about the Ogatta group, who come from another space/time dimension and who abolish distance as we know it with casual facility as they transcend our limited existence.

Emerson once wrote, "One mode of the divine teaching is the incarnation of the spirit in a form—in forms like my own." Perhaps that is why the initial stages of communications are through human channels like myself. Alien ideas are harder to accept when they emanate from an alien entity. There is also the major factor of those higher vibrational levels of energy which the ETI bring and which their channels have been trained to handle, both physically and mentally, as they walk that fine line of balance between dimensions.

When I lectured to a group of presidents of their respective companies, I spoke for close to three hours on topics ranging from ESP to ETI. As I listened to the tapes recently, I heard myself say in the opening section, ". . . and you will all go home with something of value. One third of you will believe what I am about to tell you. Perhaps a third will disbelieve. One third of you will find my experiences and facts beyond your frame of reference to believe or disbelieve. But if and when my Scenario comes to pass, all of you will remember what I said here . . . and will then meet the challenge without fear."

Such is my hope for you who read this book. Your questions will, as live-audience questions do, vary in degrees of acceptance and skepticism, but there will be a consistent degree of curiosity. "Does metal really bend?" "Is there life in other galaxies?" "Will there be land-mass shifts in the near future that will affect life on this planet?" "Are UFOs for real?" "Is the government suppressing information about life on UFOs and on other planets?" "Has there been any known contact with other civilizations from credible sources?" "Should we listen to the Ogatta group?" The list of questions is extensive and predictable.

To each of those questions I gave affirmative answers on the basis of first-hand experience and information. They are also the same questions I hear whether at university campuses as I travel around the country, or at symposiums with doctors, authors, inventors, psi researchers, or corporate executives.

We have met those who can help us technologically to make our transition from this present age into the stepped-up vibrational theater of the next phase. And heightened vibrations they will be, coupled with heightened awareness. Our experienced reality is the result of the translation of vibrations—frequencies—by our brain from the inputs of our five antennae, our senses. We lock into such a small percentage of these frequencies that in a universal sense we are practically unconscious! Many species on Earth have a higher level of perception when related to frequencies—vibrations—on a particular band. They can hear more, smell more, taste more, see more than man. If we could tune in to those frequencies, as other species are able to do, without forfeiting our abilities to interpret and relate them to other information, we would tune into a reality that is currently inaccessible to us.

Another way is open to us. Helen Keller exhibited sensory awareness in ways that we still do not understand. She demonstrated many roads to increased sentience. It remains for our technicians and scientists to unlock the secrets to this demonstrated ability so that all of mankind will benefit. When we can do this, we may be able to communicate with those beings whose very existence we deny. If and when we are without dependable supplies of electricity—essential in our present modes of communication—we shall have to rely on mental radio. Communication must be fostered to take place above and beyond our current sensory levels.

It is important to recognize the new ways of life which will open up to us, but it is also important not to let our stability be shaken in the transition. We need to learn the new rules as the time approaches. When it does come, we must stand firmly rooted, able to bend like the willow and come up with ease and grace. Each individual must be like a tree: flexible and bending to the storms of change without breaking; balanced, centered, and understanding of Nature's plan.

We must learn to share, and thus heighten the *energy* of brotherly love. We must sharpen our five senses and add to them a *sixth* sense. This sixth sense will be the springboard to a better mankind— for who would harbor evil or selfish thoughts if it was known that they could be read telepathically?

I anticipate a different but terribly exciting world in which to live, love, play, work, learn, and laugh. I look to share many bold hypotheses and technologies with those of the Ogatta group and others like them: advanced beings—entities—who will come forward to help us. As I have come to synthesize much of what I have learned, my direction has come clear. The Scenario stands: *"Due to man's inhumanity to man . . . and Nature's plan . . . there will be a change to the face of our planet."* I think about the "architects of the future" and about "glimpsing the future, not with fear but with a calm knowledge that we will help other survivors accept what Nature's dictates will be." I think about cosmic revelations which we have shared. And I think about my conclusions.

You and I are living through one of the most crucial eras to confront humanity since the dawn of history. We must meet it with a heightened sense of awareness and an inner sense of peace. I look for the American heritage of positive thrust and positive energy to assert itself in the transition. My mission will be a success if you strive to help others and allay their fears of the unknown. To quote Tauri one last time, *"Better a little light than no light at all."*

I look for the Ogatta group and similar groups to become a part of your experienced reality. I look to interfacing with those who come from the Cosmos to help Planet Earth. I look to welcoming them and assisting their benevolent efforts on our behalf. I look to the coming of the gattae.

I look to riding on a slide of light with you . . .

or without you.

AFTERWORD

Too many times in the past have I questioned the very existence of the Ogatta group. This phase inevitably comes about after a prolonged silence on their part. During one such period, I was walking down a dusty road in a remote Mexican village when a young man came strolling toward me. We passed each other and, abruptly, both of us stopped. He turned and backtracked to where I was standing and quietly asked, "Don't I know you?" My heart unaccountably began to pound as I replied, "Not really. But I feel as if we *should* know each other." The young man stared hard at me. I had to lean forward to hear him ask, "Does the name 'Oshan' mean anything to you?" Tears sprang into my eyes and spilled down my cheeks. Never had I heard the name of any of the planets in the Ogatta jorpah spoken by a stranger. The man reached out his hand, touched my wet cheek gently, and murmured, "I thought so. I thought so." He was from California.

On a trip to Shanghai, China, I spotted a student at a small table on the riverboat we had boarded for a day sightseeing. As I neared his table, our eyes met, and together we said, "I know you!" We laughed and repeated the same sentence in unison, pointing at one another. Dick and I joined him and although his English was scanty, we chatted. He had never been outside Shanghai in his entire life, and this was my first trip to China.

The Chinese "Gang of Four" had done its worst on the mentality of the students, and this one was therefore understandably reluctant and nervous about saying anything which might be misinterpreted if overheard. The recurrent thread in our dialogue was "I know you!" Our interchanges appeared to alternately stimulate and unsettle the handsome Chinese fellow.

Recalling the encounter in Mexico, I started naming the five planets of the jorpah, and when I came to Tchauvi, the confused eyes of the student suddenly widened and brimmed with unshed tears. In an uncharacteristic gesture, he put his arm upon mine. As we neared land, he detached a small pin from his lapel and handed it to Dick as a keepsake, whispering, "I know her. Your wife. I *know* her." I knew him too.

Episodes such as these are less easily described satisfactorily than one would imagine. It is difficult to articulate the experience, but they leave their mark on one's mind and consciousness. And heart. There are many human beings walking the face of this Spaceship Planet Earth who are tuned in to similar wavelengths. Psychic work can be extremely lonely. Moments of such sharing makes life—and the work—easier for the participants.

In this spirit, I have listed a dozen words from Ogatta jorpah's lexicon. If you recognize and can define any of them, you can reach me through the *S.T.A.R.* Foundation, 10 East 34th Street, New York, N.Y. 10016. *S.T.A.R.* is an acronym for Space Technology And Research, and I serve as its vice president.

coroles	peurk
krimna	piupi
lepura	raina
machet	rimz
mipul	toka
nuprey	wurcklle